G000277623

BUSHVELD *Sunset*

David James Dixon

Grosvenor House
Publishing Limited

All rights reserved
Copyright © David James Dixon, 2019

The right of David James Dixon to be identified as the author of this
work has been asserted in accordance with Section 78
of the Copyright, Designs and Patents Act 1988

The book cover is copyright to David James Dixon

This book is published by
Grosvenor House Publishing Ltd
Link House
140 The Broadway, Tolworth, Surrey, KT6 7HT.
www.grosvenorhousepublishing.co.uk

This book is sold subject to the conditions that it shall not, by way of
trade or otherwise, be lent, resold, hired out or otherwise circulated
without the author's or publisher's prior consent in any form of binding or
cover other than that in which it is published and
without a similar condition including this condition being imposed
on the subsequent purchaser.

This book is a work of fiction. Any resemblance to
people or events, past or present, is purely coincidental.

A CIP record for this book
is available from the British Library

ISBN 978-1-78623-676-0

CHAPTER ONE

Brighton March 2018

He was experiencing one of those feelings that comes along once in a while. Like the first day of Spring following a harsh winter, that feeling of fresh hope, that everything is going to be fine and that new opportunities are coming your way. He stood in the upper gallery of the church, holding the hymn book but not singing. The sun was beaming in from the stained-glass windows on the left side of the building. A ray of light seemed to pick out a man, he was an elderly black man singing in full voice and smiling. Despite this appearance, there was something that suggested the man harboured a personal sadness.

As the service concluded, he made his way down from the gallery and out onto the street, after shaking hands and exchanging a smile with the Vicar in the vestibule of the Church. Stepping onto the street he paused for a moment to take in the cool Brighton sea air and listened to the sound of the gulls, it reminded him of magical visits to the seaside as a child. Across the road, he noticed the black man from the church, he watched him turn down one of the long streets leading down to the seafront. Three youths on bicycles were following a few yards behind, they were laughing, and he instinctively sensed something was not right. One of the young boys drew level with the old man and mouthed something to him. He picked up his pace and crossed over the road to get closer. The old man was trying to distance himself from the attention he was receiving and kept his head down. The other two boys rode past the him and their friend, stopping a few yards ahead. Then they turned their bikes to face their friend and the old man. He had closed in by now and could hear that the three boys were baiting their target for a response. Suddenly, one of the boys situated up front, started riding fast toward the old man, raising his right leg and fixing it firmly, to act as a battering ram. The boy made contact and knocked him to the pavement. There was a sickening thud as the old man's head hit the pavement. The boys were laughing and slowly circling their victim, their mobile phones raised and aimed to capture the fun. They were too involved to notice him running towards them. He shoulder charged into the one that had attacked the old man and knocked the offender clean into one of the others, sending their bicycles crashing into each other. As the third one turned to him, he caught the youth square on the chin with an uppercut and knocked him off his bike. Having now taken them all out, he turned his attention to the injured victim. He leaned over the old man who was muttering a few words in a foreign tongue. After checking for injuries, he turned his head towards the boys. The recipient of the uppercut was touching his mouth and staring as his bloodied dismembered teeth on the ground, the other two boys were eyeing him, unsure of their next move.

He shouted, 'You best jog on, coz if I get up from here it will be to perform some more dental surgery on you two scumbags.'

The three of them thought better of it, grabbed their bikes and headed downhill towards the seafront, surveying the damage as they went. He turned his attention back to the old man who was clearly stunned, but on inspection had no open wounds on his skull. He rolled the old man into the recovery position and asked him if he could hear him.

'What's your name?' he asked.

The old man responded softly, 'D, D...David' as he opened his eyes.

'Are you able to stand up sir?'

'I think so.'

He helped the old man to stand up and let go of him once he was on his feet, David stumbled, he caught him and helped him over to a nearby park bench.

After a few minutes he asked, 'Do you live nearby?'

'Not far.'

'Let me take you home.'

꙳

CHAPTER TWO

Transvaal, South Africa February 1983

Sam had no idea what he was letting himself in for by signing a three-year contract to work in the platinum mines in South Africa. In spite of his young age of 23, he had travelled the world extensively during his days as a marine engineer in the Merchant Navy, but this was a completely different venture. Travelling around the world on a British ship kind of meant you never absolutely left home, this had more of a letting go feel to it. After a distasteful spell of unemployment in his industrial North East of England, he was really looking forward to the new experience, but in truth, he had no vision of what life may be like or where he would actually be living. All said though, he was prepared to take it all in his stride as a young man in need of a fresh start.

On arrival at Jan Smuts airport, Johannesburg, he was met by a representative of the Mining Company. A rather attractive Afrikaans lady, her job was to herd the new arrivals together and group them so they could be dispatched to their respective locations. His group consisted of twelve people, it looked like four of those were spouses though. It was only then that he learned he was bound for a town by the name of Rustenburg. The group was told to leave their suitcases and the Afrikaans lady instructed four black men to collect the baggage. Sam noticed that in the 10 minutes that he had been there, she was conversing in three languages. English, Afrikaans and the third, he later learned, was Tswana. Impressive.

Once onboard the minibus, the Afrikaans lady introduced herself as Hettie van 'something' and proceeded to deliver commentary during the three-hour journey, which included a stop for refreshments at what must have been the halfway point. Most of her commentary seemed to be focused on the sacrifices made and wonderful things achieved by the Voortrekkers as they pushed through the Transvaal in the early 1800's.

Despite the heat and cramped journey, the time seemed to pass relatively quickly and they eventually arrived at the town of Rustenburg. Everyone in turn was dropped off at their allocated new place of abode. For Sam, this was a camp, or single quarters, as the sign at the entrance declared. As he lay on his bed on that first night, he knew this wasn't his smartest move and that it was not going to last. He'd give it six months at the most.

Dineo was 33, single and liked his job as a minibus taxi driver, well as much as anybody with little or no alternative would do. His daily routine consisted of a 5am start, cramming as many folks as physically possible into his minibus at the township then making multiple journeys back and forth to the Rustenburg town bus stand. He would reverse the process later in the day to deliver passengers back to the township and finally park up around 9pm. In fairness it was probably what kept him going day to day, as his life other than that was very much based around surviving life in little more than a slum dwelling where human life stood for next to nothing. His sole entertainment was a weekly visit to a shebeen to numb his brain as a means of escape from his pitiful existence. Not that he knew anything different personally, he didn't, but he had seen another way of life around him, but that life was not available to him.

—᠆ᘛᘚᘘ᠆—

Sam was pretty street wise compared to most of the new arrivals to the Mining Company. He knew he could never break away if he followed their examples of settling in, which involved buying brand new cars and signing up to long term rentals of houses in affluent white areas. He chose to stay at the single quarters and took up the offer for a ride to and from the mine site with Andy, a fellow Brit that had worked in Rustenburg for a while. All Sam had to invest in was a pushbike to make it to and from the town centre where Andy would pick him up every day. The low commitment approach would work in his favour when he would come to make his break.

—᠆ᘛᘚᘘ᠆—

Kees Coetzee's family had lived and worked in the Rustenburg area for three generations. He was a shift boss on the mine which gave him and his family a good income and lifestyle. Every other week he would work the early shift, which gave him the opportunity to pick up his youngest daughter from school. School finished at 3pm which allowed Kees an hour spare to share a few cold beers with his best buddies at the tavern in the town centre. On Tuesday 23rd February 1983, he did just that, then jumped into his Bakkie and headed to the school. Five-year-old Amy loved it when Pa picked her up, he would always play his beloved Boere music at full volume during the drive home and they would clap and slap hands as they travelled home. But today she would not hear that music. Kees parked the Bakkie and went to the gates to pick up his little Bokkie, as he loved to call her. While he waited for her, a delivery vehicle parked in front of his Bakkie and its black driver started to unload his vehicle. When Kees returned, he was furious to see he had been blocked in and immediately starting shouting at the driver to 'move his fucking heap of shit and to do it now.'

The driver asked for a couple of minutes so he could finish the unloading. Kees told Amy to get in the Bakkie and wait for him. He watched her get in the passenger side then approached the driver after grabbing the tyre lever from the back of his Bakkie.

The driver took the blows to his left arm and back as he ran towards his truck and managed to escape further abuse by jumping into his vehicle and locking the door.

Kees was not finished and needed to inflict more pain on the driver. He knew that damaging the delivery truck would get this bastard fired or into serious trouble with the company he worked for. Kees jumped into his Bakkie and rammed the rear end of the delivery truck trying to create as much damage as he could with his bull bar. In his haste and temper, there was no way he could have known that Amy had got back out of the Bakkie and walked between the vehicles to pick up the school book she had dropped as she ran to get back inside. By the time Kees realised that she was not sitting next to him, the delivery driver had sped off and a crowd was gathering round the front of his vehicle. None of them had witnessed what had actually happened, but they could all see Amy's lifeless body lying on the ground.

Word travelled fast in the Afrikaans community and before long all of Kees's friends and family knew of the murder of his daughter by the black driver. Retribution would have to be swift and merciless; it was the only thing these people listened to. The bus stand was the perfect place to dish this out, there would be plenty of easy targets and amongst the confusion that would ensue, escape for the perpetrators would be easy.

Dineo's driving job was demanding, but it was better than his previous job on the farm.

In his opinion, not all whites were bad. During his time on the farm he thought that the younger generation of whites displayed the worst behaviours towards him, but they could do no wrong in their parents' eyes. They were seen as the way forward for their community, good church goers, carrying the flag for their forebears, maintaining the Boer traditions. He left that job two years previously and having less day to day contact with the whites seemed to make life a little easier for him.

It was the last run of the day for Dineo, picking up at the bus stand close to the shopping Mall rear entrance. He did not see the seven Bakkies approaching from his right side. The first thing he knew was when the bullets tore into his vehicle. He felt the pain in his right calf, but instinctively knew that worse things were happening behind him to his passengers. As usual he was over filled with day workers travelling back to the squalor of the township. By the lack of screams he knew there were not many survivors. The Bakkies had swung away from him and were delivering their fire power to several of the other parked buses. As the last Bakkie pulled away and sped off, he locked eyes with one of the gun men. They clearly recognised each other, the gun man was Jaap Van NieKirk, the son of the farmer that was his previous employer. Being a black witness to this kind of event would not fare well for him, neither with the perpetrators of the crime or the police. He had to get away from here now. Dineo opened the driver's door and jumped out of the bus. He could see that a bullet had caught him through the blood stained rip in his trousers. He would take a closer look later but for now it was run, run, run. He ran towards a parked truck that was stationed at the unloading bays at the rear of the shopping mall and climbed into its large enclosed trailer. It was partially empty and he managed to scramble between some large boxes at the far end of the storage space. He settled there and listened for sounds of anyone that could have been following him. After what seemed like an age, the large doors of the trailer were closed and the truck pulled away. To where, he had no idea, but he was safe for now.

The Kloof was a beauty spot on the edge of Rustenburg, it was the ideal spot to meet with friends and enjoy a Braai together. That is where Jaap and his cohorts had arranged to regroup. Their wives and girlfriends would already be there. The ladies had been briefed to find a good spot at the Kloof and start preparing the food. The men would be going for a couple of beers at the tavern and would collect the beer and wine for the Braai. If they needed an alibi this would help.

Dineo inspected his wound, he had been lucky. The bullet had just caught him, it had removed some flesh but that was all. He was on his way to Durban in the back of an articulated vehicle, although he did not know it yet. The driver was back loading some damaged white goods and had no stops elsewhere, so the journey would take about 12 hours in all.

Sam and Andy travelled to work the next morning, their sole topic being the massacre at the bus station. Being part of the expat community and the rumour mill within, details had emerged quickly overnight.

Estimates of the dead were sitting at an unofficial figure of 32. Of course, none of it was on TV or in the press, broadcasting of these kind of events were strictly controlled as they could have a devastating affect across the mixed communities if the wrong kind of information got out. Andy was less shocked than Sam, he had not witnessed anything like it before but events of this type were not totally unbeknown to him.

'What happens next Andy?'

'Not sure pal and unless you speak fluent Afrikaans you won't be learning anything about it at work today.'

The truck arrived at Maydon Wharf, Durban. The damaged white goods were to be offloaded, stored in a warehouse and eventually shipped back to the Far East. The big steel doors at the rear of the container were opened and Dineo heard some talking outside. Unloading wouldn't be happening for an hour as the arrival was right on lunchtime. Dineo knew the rules, he was not allowed to travel without a permit or travel pass and if caught without these, well, the consequences would not be good for him. He had to get out of the container discretely and work out a way to stay unidentified. Easier said than done, in a place foreign to him. He clambered over and navigated through the boxes and made his way to the open back doors, he looked around and lowered himself to the ground. He then scurried along the side of the warehouse until he reached the end and hid behind some large bins. What greeted him visually was both amazing and so different to anything he had ever seen before. All he had known in his 33 years was the area he had grown up in. Basically, the bushveld of the Northern Transvaal. Trees, bush, lakes and mountains. He had heard about the ocean but had never seen it. Now it was in front of him in all its splendour. Blue, so blue and huge. Ships of all colours and sizes sat along the wharf ahead of him. He looked to his left and spotted a road sign, it read Durban City Centre 6 kms. He was close to Durban, again a place he had heard of, but somewhere he thought he would never visit, but he was there now.

He had enough schooling to understand the names of the places on the backs of the many ships and recognised some of the flags, at least he knew the ones that were not South African. His mind was racing, less than a day ago he was doing his driving job in Rustenburg, now he was miles away with no idea of what to do. He pulled an empty cardboard box out of one of the bins, covered himself with it, slouched back between the wall and bins and closed his eyes.

Every country has its version of the mafia, South Africa, or more precisely, the Afrikaans community within, was no exception. The Broedebond was well placed and funded to ensure politics, business and society were managed to protect the interests of its people. Jaap and his friends were always in arms reach of its protection, when required.

Sam worked in the Rock Drill Shop, a workshop on the surface of the mine that repaired and overhauled all the equipment used by the miners who worked at the face to extract the Platinum from underground. Although his skills were relatively new in this line of work, he was an overseer of some 40 Bantu workers. They basically did all of the grunt work and he would check their output to make sure it was good enough. He wasn't at the top of the tree though, he had two Afrikaner bosses. From day one they had been nothing but kind to him. Each day they would educate him on their language and customs and he would listen to them, mainly because he had no other choice. He had no reason to dislike them, they were just blokes from a different culture but, as time went by, that culture gap seemed to widen. In the three months that he had spent working with them, he had picked up a lot of Afrikaans and the day following the massacre, they did not discuss it on any level, at least not whilst he was present.

Dineo awoke and his first conscious thought was of the shame he felt for deserting his people at the scene of the massacre. It felt like a knife in his gut, he knew this was not right, but he could not go back. It was dark now, he must have slept for 3 or 4 hours, maybe it was the shock kicking in? He was watching the workers coming and going from the ships. They were obviously changing shifts as they moved up and down the gangways. This seemed like it could be a way out for him, could he board one of these ships and get away? Maybe he could hide somewhere on board? His head was spinning with things he did not know the answer to, but he had to do something. Life under a cardboard box between a wall and bin was not the solution. Dineo walked over and joined the queue of workers at the bottom of the gangway of a large ship.

—ᴧᴧ—

'Are you sure you want to do that, you have hardly given it a go Sam,' asked Andy.

Sam laughed and replied, 'Never been so sure of anything in my life Pal.'

It had been four months and Sam had made up his mind to leave. He had seen so much of the world and had much to compare to his current set of circumstances. He was glad of the opportunity to visit this part of South Africa and take in what he did but leaving would clearly be his better choice. Nothing good was going to come of this place, at least not in his generation. The tensions he had witnessed between the cultures, the job itself and the prospect of carving out a good life here all screamed 'get the hell out.' Just how he was going to do that was another question, but the decision was made.

—ᴧᴧ—

The cover of darkness and the act of blending in with the wharfies gave Dineo a chance to find a hiding spot on the ship. He stayed on the main deck area and located a door at the front of the ship. He undid the latches and stepped inside, there were lots of heavy ropes coiled up in neat piles. He closed the door, plunging himself into darkness, the space smelled strongly of hemp and salt. He worked his way through the darkness and around the obstacles laying on the floor and found a discrete spot to hide away. The only thing that was suppressing his hunger was his fear.

—⁓—

Sam had very cleverly crafted his departure or escape from Rustenburg, he would head down to the port city of Durban, choosing a long weekend to do so. That would buy him the time he needed to execute part two of his disappearance. Resigning from his job in the conventional way was not an option, having learned from other expats that it was better to leg it rather than work out a period of notice. He took Andy's advice not to tell a soul about his plan. He didn't believe he owed the mining company anything, after all he had worked hard for them, but Rustenburg was a small place and he didn't need any complications. Sam understood how big ports around the world worked, knowing there would always be an opportunity with his background and experience to work his passage back to the UK on a deep-sea cargo ship. It may take him a couple of days in Durban, but he would eventually be able to sort something out.

'It's agreed then,' said Andy. 'We will have a send-off for you in Hillbrow and I will drop you at the airport for your flight to Durban the following morning.'

'Sure Andy, I couldn't possibly leave without standing you and your good lady dinner and a few drinks, you folks have been so kind in the time we have been together,' Sam replied, feeling quite emotional at saying goodbye to a couple of new friends that had reached out to him as a stranger in a new town.

Hillbrow was the perfect place for a send-off, it was Johannesburg's premium party spot, hotels, bars, restaurants and a great place for live music venues. Sam had a little pang of 'am I doing the right thing' based on how much he had enjoyed the Hillbrow scene. However, he put it down to novelty factor and enjoyed it for what it was. In his seagoing days this would have been just a good run ashore. Deep down inside he knew he was doing the right thing though.

Chapter Three

⚘

Brighton March 2018

It had been 3 days since the attack, Dineo opened the door and smiled, 'My friend, please come in.'

Sam stepped into the small studio apartment, 'How are you?'

'I am well, thanks to you, can I offer you some tea?' replied Dineo as he motioned towards a small table in the corner of the room.

'Yes thanks, a cup of builders will be fine' said Sam as he took a seat at the table. He turned to look out of the ground floor window onto the street, 'No lasting damage then?'

'I'll survive,' laughed Dineo.

Sam looked over at the old man's bed, neatly made up with a folded towel on the pillow, 'I am sorry you had to experience that unpleasantness.'

Dineo turned his head to look at Sam, 'I don't understand what drives kids to do that sort of thing.'

'It all seems to be linked to social media in some sick way, they use their phones to record the mayhem, then load it up to the internet,' Sam lifted his mobile phone. 'These are not just about phone calls anymore.'

Dineo smiled, 'I don't even have one of those things, I don't really need one.'

'Good for you,' laughed Sam.

Dineo poured the boiling water into the cups, 'You are not from around here are you?'

'No, neither are you I would say. In fact, I would guess you are from the North West part of South Africa?'

Dineo looked stunned and replied, 'My goodness how would you know that?'

'Because when you were coming around from your knock on the head, you were speaking in Twsana,' noted Sam. 'I worked in the mines in Rustenburg in the early 80s, I have quite an ear for languages and I picked up a bit of Tswana along with some Afrikaans and Fanagalo too.'

Sam looked at his host, noting that his hand was physically shaking as he put the teacup down in front of him.

'Who are you, why have you come here?' Dineo asked nervously.

'Whoa, hold on sir, not sure what you are thinking here. I have obviously said something that makes you feel uneasy.'

Dineo sat on the edge of his bed and waited for Sam to provide some sort of explanation to his question.

'My name is Sam. All I know about you is that I came to your aid following an attack on the street a few days ago and I brought you home, here to this apartment. I am here now because I was concerned about you,' Sam raised his hands to show his palms as he looked his host in the eyes.

Dineo calmed himself and replied, 'I am sorry, you stirred something up from my past.'

'Do you want to talk about it?' said Sam with a reassuring smile.

Dineo returned a soft look at Sam, 'Please tell me about yourself first.'

The two relaxed with their teas and Sam explained that he was from the North of England, Northumberland originally. He talked about his youth, how he had joined the merchant navy as an engineering cadet and eventually travelled the world on cargo ships for several years before being made redundant. With a lack of work prospects locally he took a job in South Africa and ended up working in the mines in the Transvaal.

Dineo interrupted politely, 'You say you were in Rustenburg in the early 80s?'

'Yes, it was early 1983, it didn't prove to be a smart move and I definitely wasn't prepared for living in South Africa at that time.'

Dineo smiled, 'I know that place well, I lived in a township close by.'

'That's incredible, what a coincidence,' Sam paused then asked. 'But why were you so shocked earlier when I suggested you were from that part of the world?'

Dineo appeared much more relaxed now, 'Let's talk about that later, but first, please tell me about your experience there.'

Sam sat forward on the small chair and placed his elbows on the table as if settling for a while, 'Sure, I felt like a fish out of water from the moment I arrived in the country. I have travelled the world and been to many countries, but South Africa was strange for me. I learned quickly that there were so many divisions. Not just the apartheid situation, there were some huge differences between the English and Afrikaans communities also. I made friends amongst the British expat community, mainly people I was working with, but I realised quickly that the lifestyle had little to offer someone like me.'

Sam paused and looked out of the window to gather more thoughts and continued.

'But what really got me was the personal discomfort I felt at how life and things in general were being controlled, do's and don'ts were everywhere and a lot of unjust things were happening.'

Dineo stood and walked towards the door of his bedsit, 'I think I would like to go for a walk, I have been cooped up in here for a few days now. Will you join me Sam?'

Sam smiled and followed, 'Sounds good to me.'

Dineo closed the door and locked it, 'So what did you do then, I mean how long did you stay there?'

Sam laughed. 'All of four months my friend, that's all I needed before I legged it out of that awful place. Oh, please forgive me, I am forgetting that this was your home. No offence meant.'

Dineo smiled at Sam, 'No offence taken and as far as it being my home, well that was never really the case, a home is somewhere welcoming, loving, somewhere safe. Believe me it was never my home.'

Sam nodded in agreement, 'Where to then David, anywhere in mind for a walk?'

'Oh, you use my English name, my real name is Dineo.'

'That's what you introduced yourself as,' a puzzled Sam replied.

'That is so my friend, you can call me either. How about a walk to The Lanes?' asked Dineo.

'Only on the proviso that you take some of the mystery out of your past and what I stirred up exactly.'

The Lanes of Brighton are a favourite haunt of many a tourist or local for that matter. Bustling narrow streets with a Bohemian feel. Situated a couple of blocks back off the sea front and main promenade of Brighton, they offer a great escape with their many pubs, restaurants and shops. Many of the pubs and cafes have outside seating which makes it a great place for people watching. It was in a Cafe just off Ship Street that Sam learned of the Rustenburg massacre from Dineo's perspective and how he had made his escape to Durban.

Sam was shocked, 'I cannot believe you were involved Dineo, this is too much of a coincidence. What happened after you boarded the ship?'

Dineo continued with his story, telling Sam that he was discovered by one of the crew within the first couple of days out to sea. They brought him before the Captain. The Captain was furious, finding a stowaway on board was bad news. As they were already in International waters and the next port of arrival was Southampton, England, the decision was made to keep going and deal with the issue on arrival in the UK.

Apparently, this decision was made easier after Dineo had recounted his story of the massacre and escape to the Captain, there was a strong case for Dineo to be classified as a Refugee or as a Stateless person in need of asylum. He told how he had received medical attention on board and was put to work for the remaining three-week sea passage, to earn his keep, so to speak. On arrival in Southampton, Dineo was handed over to the authorities for processing. The immigration officials were not so sympathetic to his case. However, once the two officials from MI6 were involved, they appeared to show more compassion. They were very interested in learning as much as they could about the apartheid regime as experienced by one of its less than fortunate citizens. They were also able to corroborate Dineo's story to a degree, based on information received from another intelligence source.

'And they allowed you to stay?'

'I was detained for three months until a decision was made, but yes I was given asylum and I have been here ever since,' replied Dineo.

🦋

CHAPTER FOUR

Transvaal, South Africa, 1996

It was never an easy task to move money or assets out of South Africa, but it became even harder after the ANC came to power. Many of the whites that were trying to escape the new regime looked to the traditional commonwealth emigration options and Australia, UK, Canada and New Zealand were the prime destinations. The family of Jaap Van NieKirk may have been asset rich at the time he made his decision to leave his beloved Afrikanerdom, but that would carry no weight should he apply to emigrate to Australia through the channels the average person may chose. Diamonds were his best option and he knew how to make them work for him, again things got tougher when the Kimberly Process was introduced to regulate and control the legitimate diamond trade, fortunately for Jaap he made his move prior to that.

It was 1996 when Jaap first broached the subject with his parents, Henny and Anneline, of leaving South Africa. They were in their mid-fifties and still enjoying a good lifestyle, despite the recent political changes in their country. His decision rocked them, not least because of the role he played on the farm, but because this would break up their precious family unit. There wasn't a day they didn't see each other. But what hurt them most was losing their only grandson, nine-year-old Andre. They adored him, he was the one that would take over the farm and carry on the Boer tradition for them. This was the hardest thing for them to take.

Jaap and his father were sitting under the jacarandas on the front porch of the homestead, it was late afternoon and the eerie orange light was beginning to appear over the bush.

'So, where do you plan to go son?'

'The natural choice would be Australia Pa, it has so much in common with life here, climate and lifestyle especially.'

'And what will you do son, how will you provide for your family?'

'Farming Pa, it's the only choice.'

'Farms are not cheap things to buy Jaap, how are you going to manage that?'

Jaap was desperate to dodge that bullet, 'I'll make a plan. Now, time for a lekker drink eh Pa?'

'Good idea son, bring the Van der Hum.'

―――――

Jaap's parents and his wife Lana, had no idea of his involvement in the massacre at the bus station in Rustenburg all those years ago. They were also blissfully unaware of the double life he had been living since his days at Wits University.

Henny and Anneline were considered outstanding members of the Boer community and highly respected for their work at the Dutch Reform Church, where they had been members for all of their lives. In their minds they were good folks, loyalty to their forebears and the church came second to nothing, other than their own family of course. They honestly believed that their Bantu farm workers were treated fairly and paid well for their services. It was not the fault of these blacks that they were born inferior, a point that was made regularly in sermons at their church. They were clearly playing their part in supporting these people in the best way they possibly could.

Jaap managed to avoid discussing any of his real plans with his father. Now the ice had been cracked, so to speak, his folks could prepare themselves for his leaving. For Jaap it was time to put step two into motion, securing the diamonds.

—–~vv~—–

The flight to Durban from Johannesburg would take just over one hour. The rugby game at Kings Park Stadium was the ideal cover for the trip. He told Lana that he was going away with some friends but he was making the trip on his own. Jaap hated Natal, not the place itself, just the people. Too many Englishmen. The Free State and the Transvaal were his domain. A two-night stay would be enough, make the contact, agree the deal and initiate the action. The cellar bar of the Beach Hotel on Durban's Marine Parade was a well known hang out for the International Mercenaries awaiting their next assignment. Primed and ready to assist with the readjustment of African affairs in many of the states to the North. Most of them had lucrative spin off businesses that supported their, risk equals benefit, lifestyles.

Penny was the barmaid that would hook Jaap up with the oke that would help resolve his issue. He descended the stairs into the dark coolness of the cellar bar, took a right turn and approached the bar, 'Een Klipdrift 'n Coke asseblief.'

The barmaid responded in English, as is often the way, single or double'?

'Groet asseblief, ben jy Penny?'

'Could be, who is asking?'

'They tell me you can introduce me to one of the Northern workers?'

'40 Rand in the tip jar, asseblief!'

Jaap dropped the rolled up notes into the tip jar on the bar.

Penny grabbed the cash out of the jar and pocketed it.

She nodded over to a blonde haired man perched on the extreme right of the bar, 'Try him bro.'

'Howzit man,' Jaap extended his hand and he approached the guy at the end of the bar.

The blonde man ignored the offer to shake and said, 'What the fuck do you want?'

Jaap took immediate offence but tried not to show it, 'Maybe nothing man.'

'Don't be shy you fuck'n' Rock Spider, take a seat.' The blonde man pointed at his drink and shouted over to Penny, 'Fill it up.'

Jaap shuffled onto a bar stool and thought better of getting into conflict, he had come a long way to engage with someone and after all he wasn't trying to hire a pussycat, 'I was hoping you may be able to help me sir, I am in the market for your services.'

'Merchandise or a living target monsieur?'

'Merchandise.'

'What currency will you be providing?'

'I'm a farmer, it will be the plant variety, enough to keep you on a high for a couple of years.'

The blonde man laughed and slapped Jaap on the back, 'I like that kind of fluid currency, tends to keep its value eh boet?' That will get you a good pocket full of glass in return.'

'Lekker. Penny, fill 'em up and take one for yourself,' Jaap turned to his new found accomplice, 'Sorry man, what's your name?'

'Serge.'

Serge had been on a death wish since he was ten years old. He was the only son of a Belgian mother and father, orphaned in the Congo, parents murdered and mother raped before his eyes. He had no other goal in life other than strike back at 'the inhuman pieces of breathing excrement' as he described his targets of hate. Durban was his place of refuge, his place of escape, but that was slowly ebbing away as yet another regime came to power to disconnect a good way of life to the promise of squalor and depravation in the name of freedom.

The two men arranged to meet the next afternoon to conclude their business, which included testing a sample of what Jaap had to offer as currency. They climbed the stairs to exit from the cellar bar and spilled out onto the busy Esplanade on the Durban seafront. The famous Golden Mile. Serge stumbled down the street to his executive room in the Four Seasons Hotel, watching passers-by as he muttered to himself, 'Bastards, fuck them all.'

———

Jaap had the perfect set up to generate untraceable cash. During his time at Wits University he had made friends with offspring of some of the wealthiest families in South Africa. He had schemed with five of these buddies and developed a very discrete operation that would hold a major stake in the marijuana and cannabis trade across South Africa and beyond. As usual, none of his close family, including his wife, ever knew of his involvement in this ongoing operation. Dagga or Zol, as it is colloquially known, was excellent currency and ideal for his purchase of the diamonds that he would eventually use to fund his exile and new life. The internal sales market was always very lucrative, however illegal export was very manageable by air and sea routes, thanks to enrolment of controllable risk takers who held low paid jobs in ports and airports. Palm greasing was both cheap and relatively safe, elimination of a risky foot soldier, although not common, could be executed with little effort. However, the utilisation of sociopathic Serge was high risk. The only saving grace, if any, was that Jaap and Serge shared many similar personality traits. Their second meeting the following day would be vital in settling Jaap's nerves on the alliance.

Serge was essentially a gun for hire. It wasn't necessarily about the money, as long as he made enough to support his drink and drug infused lifestyle away from his chosen place of work, he did not really care.

He existed mission to mission. His lack of conscience and guilt made it easy for him to consider any offer that came his way. In the main the offers usually came from foreign tinpot governments or from mining companies. They basically wanted the same thing from him, to protect their interests by eliminating anyone or anything that was challenging their cause or progress.

———

After splitting with Serge on the previous evening, Jaap made his way down to Point Road to the sleazy bars that ran alongside the wharf area. This part of town was not included on his list of Natal dislikes. He loved the randomness of the bars and how easy it was to slip in, be anonymous and indulge in the pleasures on offer. His hit list of pleasures included more alcohol, a couple of splifs of Durban poison and some female company, short term rental only. All of this could be arranged from the comfort of his bar stool. Strip shows were performed end to end. When the strippers were not stripping they were working the tables or performing other services in the tiny rooms at the rear of the property. Jaap had a very defined selection criteria for his type of girl, non-white and as cheap looking as possible. He would not remember much of his visit there or how he got home, it was purely unadulterated selfish indulgence, nothing more.

———

Jaap awoke with a babalas at 10am on day two of his visit to Durban. He didn't even make it into the king sized bed of the executive suite at the Royal Hotel, opting for a rough night on the armchair by the huge window. He would be meeting with Serge in a couple of hours, his first port of call would be the mini bar though. He opened the bottle of Castle lager and downed it in one, before taking a cold shower.

The venue for the meeting was a bar in the Malibu Hotel on the Golden Mile. The bar had great afternoon sessions with live music and was the perfect place to recover from a heavy night of indulgence. The place was already in full swing as Jaap entered and looked for Serge. Good for his word, Serge was perched at the bar and seemed to instinctively turn around and look at Jaap as he approached.

'Howzit,' Jaap said as he pulled up a bar stool and sat alongside Serge.

'Better for getting this first one down,' replied Serge as he signalled for two more draught beers to be poured.

Jaap slipped the small package of resin into Serge's pocket, 'Let's talk timing then pal.'

Serge pushed the package further into his pocket, 'Best opportunity to pick up your glass will be in three weeks time, I have a small job in Sierra Leone to attend to then.'

'That works for me man,' smiled Jaap.

'I'll be back in 10.' Serge went off to try the sample.

The place was really crowded and a comedy show group had started their routine. Most of the crowd was still half drunk from the night before which helped amplify the laughter and calls of appreciation from the audience. Jaap felt the slap to his back as Serge returned and declared, 'Half the payment up front and I need it within a week or no deal.'

'You are taking the piss, my friend.'

'I don't take the piss, my friend,' came the aggressive response from Serge.

Jaap felt a cold shiver run down his back as Serge stared him out.

'I can get you 25% next week and it will take me another week to make it up to 50%.'

Serge burst out into laughter and said, 'Well that will have to fucking well do then pal.'

'And what guarantees do I get?'

'You don't, your business need is not my primary objective, but you will get your glass. 'Now leave it at that.'

Jaap thought for a few seconds. He was wise enough to know that locating and engaging the services of someone like Serge was a rarity. On reflection, he had no option and in reality, the drugs were a replaceable commodity. Serge wasn't.

Jaap offered his hand to Serge and this time he took it, 'It's a deal.'

The path was already paved for the conversion of diamonds to laundered cash. Once again Jaap's Wits connections would ensure smooth passage for that to occur.

All he had to do was hand over the rough diamonds and within three months he would have an offshore bank account with enough capital to secure business migration to Australia.

CHAPTER FIVE

Serge was physically shattered. He was not getting any younger and at 47 he was feeling it. This had been a successful tour of duty but it had taken its toll, he was not sure how much longer he could keep this up. It had taken him three days of travel, courtesy of his hosts in Sierra Leone, just to get to Gaborone in Botswana. He would be spending the night at the Gaborone Sun Hotel, this was part of his deal. Serge could not wait to get to the room, his skin was crawling and he stunk. He threw his kit bag on the floor next to the bathroom door, ripped his filthy clothing off and jumped into the shower and stayed there for 20 minutes. Feeling suitably refreshed and clad in a large bath towel, he looked under the bed. It was there as promised, he reached under and pulled out the portable safe. He tipped it onto its back and punched in the code. A gentle ringing noise let him know that the door was now open. He lifted the box up and tipped the contents onto the bed. He opened the brown envelope first, as agreed, it contained ZAR 40,000 in used notes. Next, he picked up the keys, the car registration, not genuine of course, was shown on the attached tag and the symbol on the key let him know he would be driving a BMW 5 series back to Durban. Still dripping from the shower, he walked over to his kit bag and took out the small sack containing the rough diamonds. He threw it onto the bed, picked up the phone and called the concierge with his room service request. Sitting on the edge of the bed, he spread out the bank notes and tipped out the rough diamonds so they sat alongside each other. He let his fingers run over the top of the diamonds and spoke out loud, 'How much is this shit worth?' He knew that they would be worth next to nothing had he sold them on to the rough diamond dealers at the point where he had acquired them. But, polished and legitimised, these stones had to be worth enough to get him away from his current line of work.

He heard the knock on the door and the soft female voice declaring that room service had arrived. Serge pulled the bath towel off with his right hand and scooped the money, keys and diamonds into it with his left. He wrapped the towel into a tight ball and threw it under the bed along with the small safe. Arriving at the door just as the second knock came, he swung it open and stood there in all his glory greeting the young black beauty with a smile and 'Bonjour.'

She lowered the tray containing the six ice cold beers to check out his manhood and replied, 'I see you are well Monsieur.'

'Beers on the table, you on the bed,' replied Serge closing and locking the door behind her.

―᠁―

Lana awoke to find Jaap sitting on the end of the bed with his head in his hands, 'Are you okay dear?'

'Ya honey, just normal kak. Machinery breaking down when we need it the most. I was looking forward to the get together tonight but it looks like I will have to go to Pretoria and pick up some parts,' he replied, turning to look at her.

'Needs must my love, better we get this sorted before we leave your Mom and Pa on their own to deal with it, eh?'

'True,' he replied as he stood up and headed towards the bathroom. 'Oh, don't mention this to my folks, by the time we explain what went wrong I will have sorted the problem. Tell them that a friend needs my help and that I hope to be back to catch the end of the Braai.'

Jaap winked at himself in the mirror as he wet down his face and whispered, 'It's like taking candy from a baby.'

Serge dispensed of the young girl long before he dispensed of the six beers. His first night back from the mayhem of Sierra Leone was all about self gratification and getting a restful sleep. He had shoved her out of the room, locked the door and taken another shower before retrieving the bath towel from under the bed and placing it under his pillow. Then he took his faithful .357 from his kit bag and placed that under his pillow also.

The morning sun shone through the thin curtains and woke him at 6:30 am. He scanned the room and felt under his pillow for reassurance that things were as he had left them.

He picked up the room phone and called room service, 'Eggs Benedict, coffee and guava juice, have it sent up at 7am.'

'Would sir like a newspaper also?' came the reply.

'No, just the breakfast.'

Serge did not carry a mobile phone with him when he was on active duty, he did not trust them. He would use the hotel room phone to call Jaap for confirmation of the meeting at the agreed rendezvous point. One ring, followed two minutes later by two rings, and five minutes later by five rings.

Jaap held his phone and waited for the cycle of calls to complete. 'Ok my pal, it's on,' he muttered to himself as he walked out to his Bakkie.

The rendezvous point was the poolside bar at the Lake Motel, Hartbeespoort Dam. It would take him just over an hour to reach there from the farm, a much shorter length of time than it would take Serge to cross the border and drive down from Gaborone. Jaap had to be there first though, his plan depended on it. If he were Serge, there would be no way he would be handing over the diamonds without a further demand, irrespective of what they had agreed.

—⁓—

Serge headed to the car park at the front of the hotel, located the Beamer and threw his kit bag on the back seat. He divided the diamonds and placed them into two small plastic bags, sealed them and placed them in the window wash container, clicked its cap back into place and closed the car bonnet. Climbing into the vehicle he taped his gun under the passenger seat and opened the glove box. Everything was there, false ownership and insurance papers for the car, fake drivers' licence and a forged passport to match the names on everything else. He wouldn't be keeping this vehicle though, it would be repossessed in Durban. 'Shame,' he said out loud as he pulled away and headed towards the South African border. He couldn't get the thought of double crossing Jaap out of his mind, but he came back to the same problem every time. He did not have a fence for the diamonds and without one they would only be worth a fraction of their true value. Still, he was holding them so he had bargaining power.

—◆—

Jaap arrived at the rendezvous point two hours before the meeting was due to take place. He would not be parking his Bakkie in the motel car park, instead he chose to leave it in a parking space over the road at the Snake and Animal Park. He would spend an hour mixing with the tourists there and then position himself to observe the arrival of Serge.

—◆—

Serge made it through the border point without any issues and, as he headed out of Kopfontein, he pulled the car off the road and recovered the diamonds. He would have to present them to Jaap to enable an effective discussion about not handing them over.

—◆—

Jaap had brought enough Xylazine to kill a horse and had two methods of administering it, orally and intra-muscular by dart. If he needed to use the sedative, the situation would decide the size of the dose. It was time to take up a vantage point near the car park for the Motel. He crossed the road and headed up to a secluded high point to ensure he would not be detected. Twenty minutes later a BMW 5 series coated in red dust pulled into the car park and swung around to park under the shade of a tall tree. The driver side door swung open and out stepped Serge. He stretched, looked around the car park and walked around to the passenger side of the car. It was clear to Jaap that Serge was recovering something from under the passenger seat and Jaap was sure he knew what it was. Serge had a small satchel strung over his left shoulder, he rested his hand on the strap as he locked the car and walked up towards the pool bar. Jaap thought about letting the air out of one of the rear tyres and decided not to. He wouldn't need to do that he reassured himself, almost laughing at the amateurish ploy. He placed the rifle loaded with the Xylazine under the tree at his vantage point and headed back down to the car park and then up to the pool bar.

Serge was sitting on a bar stool attempting to chat up the young waitress. Jaap almost felt a pang of respect as he eyed his partner in crime, after all, this oke was an achiever.

Serge spotted Jaap approaching from the reflection in the mirror behind the bar. 'That'll be two draught beers please Sarah,' he called to the waitress.

'Coming up,' she replied.

Jaap nodded at Serge, 'Baai Dankie, boet.'

'Geen problem nie,' responded Serge.

Jaap parked off on the bar stool next to Serge, 'You made it then?'

'Never a problem pal.'

'And the glass, you managed to get it?'

'Fuck man, you haven't even picked your fucking beer up yet.'

'There's a lot resting on this Serge, do you have them?' Jaap altered his approach and lifted his beer with a salute to Serge.

'Ya man, relaxez vous. Stress is a killer boet,' Serge mirrored the salute with his raised beer.

They retired to a table close to the pool which gave them the privacy they needed as well as a clear view of the mountain that overlooked the motel.

'This place is lekker hey,' said Jaap

'Shame, how it's going to change though,' offered Serge in return.

'That's why I need the glass, it's my ticket.'

'And what about my fucking ticket? I am the one taking the risks so you can pave your golden passage out of here.'

'We had a deal Serge,' Jaap noticed the change in mood and the intense stare of Serge's blue eyes.

'Well that deal is off pal, the landscape has changed. What I am holding for you is worth a shit load more than what you are offering.'

Jaap sat back in his chair and took a deep controlled breath, he had to make the right call on his plan. Serge was already confirming the need for the Xylazine.

'Okay Serge, I hear you, tell me what you are thinking,' Jaap put on his negotiation face.

'I need to fund my retirement, Seychelles or Mauritius, I don't really care, but these days are coming to a close for me and you can help me get out.'

'Show me the stones Serge, I need to see what you came back with.'

Serge laughed at Jaap, 'Nice try man.'

'Seriously Serge, these are rough diamonds man. I have no idea what you have brought back. Plus there will be many payoffs before they reach a dollar value for me.'

Serge placed his right hand into his satchel and simultaneously placed his left hand under the back of his shirt.

'You wouldn't man,' said Jaap moving his head to acknowledge the reach for the gun.

'What do you fucking take me for man, I do this for a living. There's only one witness here and the waitress bitch will go if you pull any strokes man. Understand?'

'Sure.'

All Jaap had to do was see the diamonds for now, he knew enough about rough diamonds to be able confirm that there were sufficient to justify going to phase two of his plan. Serge removed his left hand from his back, without the gun. He stared at Jaap as he did so. He had sent a clear enough message for now. He placed the satchel on the table and flipped it open then carefully tipped the diamonds onto it. Jaap held in a smile, there were enough, but not to share.

Serge smiled at Jaap, 'So?'

'So, I say we have another drink to celebrate,' said Jaap as he stood up and walked towards the bar. He would have to judge precisely how much Xylazine to tip into the beer glass, he needed Serge to be conscious for at least ten minutes. Jaap chose his moment carefully to make his move. Serge was looking in the satchel and Sarah had her back to him when he administered the sedative.

He walked back to the table and placed the beer in front of Serge, 'It will take some time to get the money to you. You realise that hey?'

'How much money are we talking?' replied Serge, taking a large drink from the doctored glass.

Jaap knew his reply did not matter, 'I would say at least US$150,000.'

'That will do nicely and worth waiting for,' said Serge as he clinked beer glasses with Jaap.

Jaap looked at the satchel as if to suggest that Serge hand over the diamonds.

'You do know what will happen if you double cross me man?' Serge responded coldly.

'Ya, I do,' nodded Jaap, knowing that he already had. 'You heading back via Pretoria?'

'Yes, I may overnight there,' said Serge as he handed the diamonds to Jaap.

'Probably a good idea, you are looking a little tired.'

Serge nodded and rubbed his eyes. The effect of the Xylazine was starting to kick in. Serge's eyelids were starting to droop and his jaw appeared a little slack.

Jaap offered his hand to Serge, 'I will be in touch, give me a couple of weeks. How about we meet up in Durbs again, same place?'

'Lekker,' replied Serge shaking hands with Jaap.

Jaap watched Serge head down to the car park. He gave a smile and a thumbs up to Sarah and headed off to recover his rifle and monitor Serge from his vantage point. Serge climbed into the car and rested his head on the steering wheel for a few seconds. He sat up straight and went to pull his seat belt on but didn't make it, he fell forwards on the steering wheel. Jaap watched for two minutes to make sure he was out for the count, then proceeded down to the car and climbed in the passenger seat. Serge was salivating and his breathing was very shallow.

'Perfect,' Jaap muttered to himself as he reached over and took the gun from the back of Serge's pants. He looked in the glove box and found the false documents. 'How convenient,' he laughed to himself and he put them back. Then he pulled Serge's head back, opened his mouth and poured in the rest of the Xylazine.

Jaap got out of the car and pulled Serge across to the passenger seat, then got into the driver's side and drove over to the Snake and Animal Park. He transferred the guns and Serge's kit bag into his Bakkie, jumped back into the Beemer and drove off east along Scotts Road, hugging the edge of the massive lake. He knew this place well, a kilometre up the road would be the perfect place for the ditch. Jaap stopped the car, switched of the engine and opened all of the windows. He watched and listened for a few seconds. When he was sure that no vehicles were approaching, he started the engine and pulled off the road onto a steep incline on the lake side. He got out and pulled Serge back into the driver's seat, placing the seat belt on him. He wedged Serge's foot onto the accelerator pedal and moved round to the passenger side, started the engine and put the automatic lever into drive. The car was screening at high revs.

'Kak,' Jaap shouted, he had not released the hand brake. With his feet outside, he leaned over the passenger seat and released the hand brake. The car immediately lurched forward with Jaap still in it. It took him all of his strength to push himself out. He fell clear of the car as it raced off towards the lake. He looked around to make sure that no one had witnessed his deed.

'Safe travels boet,' he shouted as he watched the car enter the water at speed.

It only took seconds for the car to totally submerge into what was a deep part of the lake.

'Tot siens,' Jaap said as he dusted himself down and headed up the incline and back along the road towards his Bakkie.

No one would miss the man who had lived his life as Serge Dubois and died as Piet Botha, owner of a BMW 5 series car.

—⁓—

One week later and the diamonds were bound for Antwerp where they would enter the diamond pipeline. Although the value would increase considerably after cutting, faceting and polishing, Jaap would only receive payment based on the rough diamond value minus the cost for the payoffs. His share would amount to US$240,000. After Jaap had passed over the diamonds to the handler they were smuggled into Jan Smuts airport and given to a contact in the baggage handling area for South African Airways flights bound for Amsterdam. An accomplice would skilfully unpick the stitching on the leather suitcase handles belonging to Mnr en Mev Jan Kelders. He would pack the diamonds into the handles and resew them to look absolutely normal.

Mnr en Mev Jan Kelders would report their baggage as missing at Schiphol Airport and would receive their baggage intact at their hotel twenty four hours later with a written apology from the airline. By then the diamonds would have been extracted from the handles and delivered to the final contact in Antwerp, Belgium.

—◦m◦—

Three weeks later and Jaap's offshore bank account was looking very healthy and he would begin the process of business migration to Australia.

✿

CHAPTER SIX

Narrogin, Western Australia 1997

This was prime farming country, the climate was similar, the homestead was similar, but still Lana would shed her tears alone each afternoon for the first six weeks they lived in the West Australian wheat belt town of Narrogin. It was hard for her to understand why her wonderful Jaap wanted to start a new life here. All their family and friends were in the Transvaal. Yes, things were changing in South Africa, but the Afrikaans community was strong, they weren't about to abandon the years of struggle that their Boer forebears had sacrificed so much for, it was not the right thing to do. Surely whatever changes were to come would be met with stiff resolve by her people.

Now they were in a different country with different values and interests to anything they had grown up with. It was a major reset for her and it was difficult. She had no one to talk to and certainly would not let Jaap into her world of concern and disappointment. He was the love of her life and she would not do anything to jeopardise their wonderful loving relationship. He was her man.

Jaap did not hold the same views, dark triad personality types weren't usually that emotionally driven. Yes, there was a time when she meant a lot to him, but after the birth of the son he so much craved, that seemed to fall away all too fast. Control, manipulation and lack of empathy was his stock in trade.

It didn't take Jaap long to establish himself within the local farming community.

He knew how to farm and was well versed at engaging with decision makers and influential types. Once again, that was not that important to him, the farm was only a front anyway.

Things were going well for 10-year-old Andre. Thanks to his proficiency at both cricket and rugby, he was fitting in well at school. He had a funny accent but at least he wasn't another bloody Pom.

One day, Andre came home early from school to find his mom having her afternoon weep. 'Don't worry mom, things will be okay,' he tried to comfort her. Lana hugged him and told him she was having a bout of woman's blues, nothing for him to worry about. Andre patted his mom on the back, 'I miss home too Mom.'

In 1997, the drug scene was changing rapidly. Social poisons of choice were changing to designer pills and substances that could be taken without drawing too much attention to the act of taking them. Northbridge, with its late night bars and clubs, was the market place for these new party drugs. It only took Jaap a short time to identify the dealers and pushers and to trace back the supply lines. He decided his best way to approach this was to find the person at the top and negotiate a way in.

He had plenty to offer on the logistics side of things as well as having a glittering track record of not being detected whilst running a national operation. How could they refuse him? Within nine months, Jaap had established a small slice of the action and was on his way to bigger things.

―⁓―

Lana and Jaap took coffee on the front porch as the sun rose to the east of the homestead, throwing an orange light onto the surface of their huge wheat silos that are so prevalent across the West Aussie wheat belt.

'But Lana, you must make an effort, nothing comes easy in life. We are doing this for the future of our son, stop dreaming about our past life in S.A, that is over, this is the future for us here and now.'

Jaap retracted his arm almost as quickly as Lana placed her hand on it.

'I am sorry honey, you are working so hard for us. I just miss the family and our friends so much,' she replied.

'They can come see us any time they like.'

She tried to hug him and he responded by patting her on the back, 'now I have to get ready for the trip to Perth tomorrow Hun.'

'Do you want us to come with you? It would be nice to have some family time there.'

Jaap smiled, 'maybe next time dear, I've so much running around to do this trip.'

―⁓―

The main road in Kalgoorlie is Hannan Street, named after the gold prospector Paddy Hannan. Hannan was responsible for the gold rush that descended upon the desert town in 1893 and, years after his lucrative find, he has remained a local folk hero. Hay Street runs parallel to Hannan Street and is the infamous vice hotspot in the mining town of Kalgoolie. Many a hard earned dollar of the mine or construction workers would be blown in one of the many establishments in that part of town. Scantily glad lovelies would display their wares and ply their trade to passers-by as they leaned against the corrugated frontages of the brothels.

This was always the first port of call for Jaap on his pseudo business trip. He would phone ahead to arrange three girls and a hot tub to coincide with his arrival, following his six hour drive from Narrogin.

There was never a need for him to visit Perth for his other line of business, after all it was best if he did not set foot in Northbridge. All dealing could be adequately managed from the town affectionately known as Kal. He would laugh out loud to himself as he drove his Ute, the Aussie equivalent of the Bakkie, along the long stretches of nothingness between his new home and his secret playground. Sometimes he had to pinch himself, as it was hard to believe just how good he was at working people to get what he wanted.

The madam, Sandra, ushered him through to the executive suite, 'Fill your boots mate, when you are done we will have a beer and our talk.'

'Hello to you too darling,' he replied.

Jaap's boots wouldn't be filled until dawn which pissed Sandra off a lot as he was utilising three of her finest assets free of charge.

'You're robbing me blind you bastard,' she shouted at him as she woke him with an ice cold beer at 8am.

He rubbed his eyes and grabbed the beer from her, 'Small price to pay for what I bring to you Sandra, you have never had it so good.'

The set up was simple, Jaap would provide the base products, Sandra would arrange for them to be transported to the lab located in the bush outside Coolgardie for processing. Jaap would receive the finished product in fertiliser bags at his farm and redirect the merchandise to the onsellers that worked the Northbridge outlets. Liquid cash would come back to the brothel, where it would be cleansed. Jaap and Sandra would pick up high quality second hand farm equipment from struggling farmers for cash and would resell it on as legitimate partners from their agricultural equipment dealership.

Jaap sat up and took a long swig of this beer, 'I believe Fremantle may offer us some opportunity to expand our little operation?'

Sandra sat at the foot of his bed, 'Careful there mate, there's a reason I haven't ventured there before now.'

'Why?'

'Let's just say that place is managed by others that we don't want to upset,' she warned.

'Surely a little competition could be a good thing though?' he responded.

'It would be more conflict than competition mate.'

'Why don't we try a small sample, test it out eh?' he wasn't about to give up that easy.

'Look mate, if you do, then you do it without me, no way I am getting involved.'

'Okay, okay, keep your drawers on.'

'They've been firmly locked on for a while now mate,' she laughed.

They spent the next hour discussing their joint business matters.

———

The second port of call for Jaap would be a visit to the lab just outside of Coolgardie to make sure his standards were being met to avoid detection. He would rest up until the heat of the afternoon had subsided before driving out of Kalgoorlie. As he drove south west on highway 94 he admired the Jacaranda blooms that lined both sides of the road. It made him think of the trees shaded the front of his parents' farm.

He had reset his odometer as he left the brothel to make sure he would pick up the bush track at the 30 kilometre point, resetting it once more as he turned on to the bush track. The lack of landmarks in the bush made it difficult to find the location of the lab without some props. Six kilometres onto the track he would slow down and look right until he picked up the faded blue car bonnet five meters in from the edge of the track. If the bonnet was turned upside down, he would abort the visit, if not he would carry on for 300 meters, pull the Ute off the road and park it at 45 degrees to the track. He would then tie a rope to the middle of the roo bar and walk out 40 meters maintaining a 45 degree angle to the Ute. From that point he could see the entrance to the underground lab. The surrounding landscape always looked the same, dark red earth, scrub and some scattered trees no more than two meters tall. Any sounds heard would come from the small birds which populated the area. The lab was no more than a tunnel, four meters deep and three meters diameter running a length of ten meters. It had been designed to give some natural air movement and ventilation.

Jaap dropped the beer can full of pebbles into the entrance to summon the technicians at work. The visit would be short but long enough to hand over the envelopes containing a cash bonus that helped to buy the silence and loyalty of the two guys employed to manufacture the product.

Despite being in a very remote location, Jaap would deliberately keep his voice low and ask, 'All good fellas, any problems?'

The response would always be the same, thumbs up and a smile obscured by a protective respiratory mask.

The chance of detection by the authorities was low. In reality, it would be more likely for the lab to be discovered by tourists using metal detectors, trying their hand at some prospecting. But Jaap was very strict on maintaining his standards and his workers knew that.

Following the brief visit, Jaap would retreat to his Ute walking backwards, using the rope to whip across the red dust to cover any tracks that he may have made. Then it was back to Kalgoorlie.

This time he would book a night at the Exchange Hotel to experience some different fun in the mining town. His alternative entertainment included drinks in the many topless bars and a visit to the two up school. The old traditional game of two up was held inside an iron corrugated shed on the outskirts of the town. The cool desert evening was a welcome contrast to the heat of the day and the burning night sky was a reminder of happier times in his homeland.

CHAPTER SEVEN

※

Jaap could make out a red car parked in front of the homestead even though he was almost a kilometre away. He had just finished his late afternoon rounds on the farm and was heading home to Lana and Andre. Lana would be preparing dinner and Andre would more than likely be doing his homework. Smart kid, he thought to himself. As he reached the gravel parking area he could now see that they had a visitor. A young man was chatting with Lana and he had his hand on Andre's shoulder. Andre was looking up at the young man and smiling, almost admiring him. Jaap parked the Ute and eyed the young man before saying hello to them all.

Lana broke the silence excitedly declaring, 'Jaap honey, your friend Goran has come to visit. Andre has just been for a spin is his beautiful car. Isn't it lovely?'

Jaap was furious and found it hard to speak, he took a deep breath and replied, 'It's a beauty, Goran good to see you, howzit?'

Goran smiled and extended his hand to shake with Jaap, 'Always a pleasure to meet up with a good friend, how are you Jaap? I thought we could pop into town to the tavern for a cold beer and a chat about the new business idea you have. Okay?'

'Sure,' replied Jaap still trying to compose himself.

'My car or yours mate?' Goran's accent was a mix of Aussie and Croatian.

'Let's take mine,' replied Jaap nodding towards the Ute. 'We won't be long honey. Goran won't be joining us for dinner though. Andre, I am sure Goran won't mind you playing inside his car, eh mate?'

Goran smirked back at Jaap, 'Not a problem mate.'

As soon as the doors closed on the Ute, Jaap turned to face Goran, 'Who the fuck are you and what makes you think you can approach my family in this way?'

Goran calmly kept looking straight ahead at the road and replied, 'Easy mate, what kind of way is that to greet a potential new business partner?'

'I said who the fuck are you, answer my fucking question you fucking prick.' Jaaps' hands were shaking as he gripped the wheel, trying to steady them.

'Relax mate, all in good time,' said Goran, this time with a stern look at Jaap.

No more was said until they reached the front bar of the Narrogin Tavern, a typical federation style timber building, painted green and cream and built on a wide crossroads in the centre of the tranquil farming town.

'Shit, looks like I left my wallet in the car, mine is a midi of draft mate,' Goran stared expressionless at Jaap.

Jaap ordered the drinks and placed his wallet on the beer mat in front of him as is the tradition in many West Aussie bars. 'Okay, explain mister, or you will be drinking the next beer through a hole in your throat.'

'Sandra told me you could be an awkward piece of work.'

'Sandra?'

'Yes, madam Sandra, she is a mutual friend,' Goran was doing a good job of pushing Jaap's buttons trying to get a reaction.

Jaap was getting nervous now, he had managed to keep a lid on his little arrangement with Sandra from his family for almost a year now. Yet here was a stranger, an intimidating one at that, who may well know everything about him. This bastard had crossed a line by going to his house and having direct contact with his wife and son. 'Think Jaap, think,' he was saying to himself.

'Okay Goran, let's back up the truck here.' Jaap took a long swig of his chilled beer. 'What's the story pal?'

Goran smiled at Jaap, 'I know all about your business with Sandra, the lab, how you get your feedstock, how you market your product and also how keen you are to step on the toes of me and my associates.'

'That fucking bitch,' Jaap drained the last of his beer and nodded to the barman to pour two more.

'That fucking bitch is the only reason you did not die in a farming accident yesterday mate, which by the way could still happen unless you chose to cooperate with us.'

'Who the fuck is us?'

'Let's just say we are a major provider of entertainment and pleasurable substances in the Fremantle area,' Goran picked up his second beer and nodded his appreciation to Jaap.

'Got it man,' Jaap laughed out loud, 'so what does cooperation mean, Goran?'

'Oh, I think the first step for you is to pay us a visit, come and enjoy some of our Balkan hospitality. Yes, that would be the first step mate.'

'When?'

'I have your number, I will text you within a couple of days. Bring a toothbrush and change of underwear. No need to bring your good lady or that charming boy of yours, if we need to see them, we know where they are.'

Jaap was palpable, he was not used to being controlled by anyone, he was the one that did the controlling. Nobody threatened his family!

Goran could see how much he had wound Jaap up, it took him all of his time not to burst out laughing, 'Okay, I think we have reached a good point to head back now, let's hope your boy hasn't become too attached to my car mate.'

The text arrived two days later. *You are checked into the Esplanade Hotel this Friday. The bill is prepaid. Easy on the mini bar. Will pick you up at 9pm.*

Jaap did his usual job of explaining away the reason why a family visit was not a good idea. Toothbrush, undies and .44 magnum packed, he headed away from the farm again, but this time a little unsure of what waited for him at the other end. In a way he was looking forward to it, he had to gain back control. Getting mugged off by these jokers stung like a snake bite.

He arrived in good time and parked off at the lobby bar at 8:45pm. 'Double brandy and coke please.'

The dining room adjacent to the bar area was full, a mix of tourists and locals he assumed. He scanned around discretely to see if anyone was checking him out. There didn't seem to be.

He was just about to order one more drink when Goran tapped him on the shoulder and smiled, 'Settle up mate, we will be taking care of things for the rest of the evening.'

It was only a short walk before they reached the Cappuccino strip, the premier cafe and restaurant area of the port City of Fremantle. Goran led Jaap to an alfresco table occupied by three men enjoying the cool evening air. Jaap checked them out, two of them looked to be over 50 and another one that must be about the same age as Goran, he guessed 28.

They stood and smiled offering their hands 'Kaku si.'

Jaap respectfully shook hands and took a seat at the table.

One of the older gentlemen at the table said, 'So nice of you to join us this evening Mr Van NieKirk.'

'So nice I am able to, apparently.' quipped Jaap.

Laughter burst out around the table.

Goran placed a glass in front of Jaap and poured a shot of Grappa into it from the carafe that was sitting in the centre of the table, 'Please, drink with us. Dobro Zdravlje.'

Jaap responded, 'Gesondheit,' wondering when he would get the opportunity to understand why he had been summoned and what the evening would hold.

One of the older men spoke, 'Introductions. I am Branko, this is my brother Kris, this young man is Luka and I believe you already know Goran.'

Jaap responded with a nod to each as they were introduced, 'So why have you brought me here gentlemen?'

Branko looked at the others and answered, 'As you already know it was brought to our attention that you were eyeing a corner of our trade here, that won't be happening. But you are a person of interest to us, you clearly have skills and we want to explore the opportunities for future business.'

Goran poured another round of Grappa and Branko continued, 'We have a working arrangement with Sandra, we respect each other's spaces. We have known about you since you imported your first shipment of raw product. This is a small town Mr Van NieKirk.'

Jaap downed his shot of Grappa, 'So why have we not met before now?'

Branko sat forward and lowered his voice slightly, 'No need, besides we needed to know how discretely you could run your business, what products you were introducing and who is in your network. We knew it was only a matter of time before you tried to make a move on our patch and that was our signal to intervene.'

'So, what is next?' asked Jaap.

'You will be our guest this evening, dinner, a visit to our night club and, if all goes well, a short cruise on our yacht to watch the sunrise,' Branko smiled and drained the last of the Grappa into the five glasses.

Jaap excused himself to use the bathroom. He was quite pleasantly surprised by the turn of events. This may not be such a bad thing. He placed his forearm on the wall, rested his forehead on it and leaned over the urinal. He could feel the effects of the Grappa already. Perhaps it was mixing with the adrenaline pumping through his veins.

He didn't hear Luka enter the bathroom, as he zipped up he turned to see him blocking the exit.

Luka smiled, 'Just a short security check, if you don't mind?'

Jaap raised his arms above his head and was glad he had decided not to carry his weapon. It was a close thing though.

It was 1am by the time dinner was done and they made their way to the night club. Entry was via the main entrance, the Croats liked to be seen going to the front of the queue, making their presence felt by the revellers patiently waiting in line. By now Jaap was feeling the effects of the Grappa and wines that had been in plentiful supply during the prolonged dinner. The night is still young for these folks he thought, best pace himself from now on. They were led to a table in the private VIP area which was roped off in a section overlooking the dance floor. Six bottles of Champagne on ice adorned the circular table. The music was loud and for much of the next hour coherent conversation was limited. Goran had been missing for twenty minutes or so before he returned to the VIP area with four young girls. He organised them so they were scattered into seats between Jaap and each of his Balkan hosts. Jaap had noticed the girls earlier gyrating themselves around the dance floor, flirting and teasing with everyone, including themselves. It appeared that they had been hand-picked by Goran. Branko placed his arms around the shoulders of the girls sitting either side of him and in turn whispered something to them. In response the girls leaned forward of Branko, laughed and gave each other a high five. Whatever he had said to them had clearly met with their approval. One of the girls stood up, topped all of the glasses with Champagne and passed Branko's message on to the other two girls. Kris raised his glass and they all toasted whatever the plan was.

Jaap leaned across to Goran and said, 'What's the cause for celebration?'

Goran replied, 'The girls will be joining us on our morning cruise.'

Half an hour later they all stood up, the girls and Jaap were ushered outside via a rear entrance. The Croats left by the front entrance of the club then made their way to the rear via an alleyway. The girls and Jaap had already been loaded into a black stretch Limo and were busy serving up the chilled champagne that was waiting for them on the small central table. The Limo driver waited for the other men to board, he didn't require any instruction for the destination, he had done this run several times prior. It only took a few minutes to reach the Fremantle Marina. The girls could hardly contain themselves when they saw the yacht, reactions ranged from stunned silence to whoops of joy.

Luka did his best to reduce the noise, telling them that people were sleeping on the other yachts around them, 'Respect ladies please.'

All boarded, they pulled away and headed out to the western bays of Rottnest Island. The rohypnol was administered to two of the girls somewhere along the way to Rottnest.

Kris was sitting on the fore deck with Jaap looking out at the calm ocean in front of them, 'How are you Jaap, I hope you are enjoying yourself?'

Jaap was feeling relaxed, enjoying the buzz, 'Ya, good thanks Kris.'

'That's great mate, you do understand there is no such thing as a free lunch though?'

Jaap wondered when this conversation would come, 'Sure. So what's this going to cost me?'

'No cost, just a small demonstration of where your loyalties lie,' Kris placed his hand on Jaap's shoulder, 'head down to the cabins below, Goran will let you know what's going to happen next.'

Jaap made his way aft and arrived at the entrance to the deck below.

Branko was waiting and opened his arms to invite an embrace, 'Jaap, you have settled our nerves my friend. We hope we can do business together in harmony.

Meanwhile we have a gift for you waiting below. Enjoy my friend.'

Jaap released himself from the hug, smiled and headed down the ladder to the cabin, 'You have been so kind Branko and doing business together in harmony is everything I could wish for.'

As he descended, he could see two of the girls hugging, kissing and laughing with Luka on the rear seating area of the yacht. Jaap was slightly apprehensive about what awaited him but did have a feeling that the worst was over. Whatever the gift was he knew he had to accept it. He was now genuinely thinking that a slice of action in the Fremantle area was a possibility. This could be great, he had done is homework. For six months of the year passenger boats were regular visitors to Fremantle, the potential for sales was massive.

Goran was waiting for him and as Jaap approached, he pushed a cabin door open.

'Your gift awaits you mate,' Goran slapped Jaap on his back and ushered him into the cabin.

The lights had been dimmed, soft music was playing on the speakers spread throughout the yacht and two naked drugged teenage girls were lying on the bed for his pleasure.

Jaap said nothing, he just looked back at Goran with an appreciative smile and entered the cabin. Goran closed the door and Jaap heard the key clicking. So good of them to respect his privacy to accept his gift, or was it an initiation ceremony? By now he did not care.

CHAPTER EIGHT

The package arrived at the farm five days after the visit to Fremantle. Jaap discovered it on the passenger seat in his Ute, it must have been placed there overnight. He cautiously opened it. It contained a VHS video and an A4 envelope. He opened the envelope and tipped out the contents onto the passenger seat. There were several photographs and a smaller envelope. He picked the items up. The first photo was an image of him leaving the night club, he was laughing and had his arm around two of the girls. The second, a shot of him inside the club, only showing him with two girls at a table with Champagne glasses raised. The third was an image of him with the girls on the yacht. He slid his finger along the flap of the smaller envelope and pulled out two pieces of paper. One was a receipt for the hire of a yacht, naming him as the person that made the hire. The second was a newspaper article concerning a claim of date rape that had occurred on the previous weekend in Fremantle. By now he was putting it all together and just knew what would be on the video.

'Bastards,' he cried out to himself, clenching his fist and banging it into the steering wheel. This could not be happening to him.

Two days later and he was still in a permanent state of rage. He wanted to finish Sandra. She was responsible for this, his plans were going well until she dropped him in it with the Croats. He couldn't concentrate on anything else. But, he was gridlocked. If anything happened to her the Croats would act, their threat was clear. He was at their mercy now. As much as it tore at him, he had to sit still, wait and bide his time until the opportunity came to gain back control.

Three days after the package, the message pinged on his phone. *Kal, Exchange Hotel. Thursday 6pm. Be in the sports bar!*

Lana had been chewing at his ear for weeks now, she felt she needed to be more involved in something. One of her friends had suggested that they open some Tea Rooms in Narrogin town centre.

'Okay, how much do you need for this?' Jaap responded to her idea, thinking this could be a good way to keep her distracted and less interested in his current affairs.

'Does that mean yes honey?'

'I guess so.'

Lana hugged him, 'Thank you so much Jaap.'

He responded with a simple peck on her cheek, 'Okay Lana.'

Thursday came and he made his way to Kalgoorlie. Multiple screens placed around the bar were displaying Aussie rules football and cricket games that were being played at various venues around Australia. He had arrived early and was trying to pick a place at the bar that wasn't over occupied by middle aged Aussie blokes clad in shorts, singlets and thongs. He found a spot at the edge of the bar close to a side entrance, thinking that he may need that.

'Midi of Emu Bitter,' he requested of the topless barmaid.

As she poured it she smiled at him, hoping to attract a small tip, which he in turn threw into the tip jar to his right.

'Thanks mate let me know if you need anything else,' giving him a wink as she rubbed a piece of ice on her nipple.

'I'll let you know,' he replied.

True to form, his visitor arrived bang on time and it was exactly who he thought it would be.

'Jaapie pal,' said the smiling Goran.

Jaap did not respond, he just stared back. Goran sidled up next to Jaap, all the time smiling at the topless lovely.

'You have the floor,' said Jaap attempting to be a cool as he could muster.

'Got yourself in a little spot there pal. I thought you might have been a bit smarter. Then again, we did our research. Sandra helped us and let us in on some of your apparent weaknesses.'

'Let's cut to the chase mate, what the fuck do you want from me?'

Goran looked Jaap straight in the eyes, 'You really need to learn how to talk to people with a civil tongue my friend. The universe doesn't spin around you mate.'

Jaap stared back for a second then looked at his beer, 'Please, go ahead.'

'That's better, we are willing to overlook your incursion into our space but there is a price,' Goran downed the remainder of his beer and signalled the ice queen to pour two more. 'We have a healthy trade in Freo and the Southern suburbs but have yet to break into the Cruise ship market. That's mainly down to the fact that what we deal in is easily detectable. We would like to expand into something closer to your product range.'

'Ah, so why didn't you talk about that in Fremantle last weekend?'

'Because my Uncle Branko wasn't about to sell out to someone that has been in the country five minutes. He has worked hard to establish our business. He needed a good bargaining position, we believe we have that advantage now.'

'What's to stop me walking away and calling your bluff?'

Goran pulled his mobile phone out of his pocket, put it on speaker and dialled a number. It rang three times before it was picked up.

'Goran, what the hell are you doing calling me on a family day mate, I'm trying to watch the footy.'

The voice was instantly recognisable to Jaap, it was his Northbridge bent cop.

Goran smirked at Jaap and replied, 'Sorry Mick, just want to know that you received the brown paper envelope and that our rapist friend is lined up for a visit.'

'Too bloody right mate, when have I ever let you down?'

'All good then Mick, thanks and enjoy the footy.'

Goran turned the phone off and looked at Jaap, 'Mick's a double dipper mate, always has been. But we are confident that he knows where his real loyalties lie. You still feel the same about walking away Jaapie?'

'So, what's the deal?'

'Business as usual for you and Sandra, but with an increased production of 100%. The extra merchandise is diverted to us and you guys will take a 30% share of our sales.'

'That's 30% each,' snapped Jaap.

Goran laughed, 'Love your South African humour mate. This is a take it or take it offer. You two will share the 30%.'

'And the contents of the package?'

'Agree to this now and all of that unpleasantness disappears.'

'How can I trust you?'

'You can't, but I don't see that you have any other option.'

CHAPTER NINE

Brighton April 2018

It was a couple of weeks since Sam and Dineo had enjoyed their chat at The Lanes. Sam felt that there were still conversations to be had about the massacre and how Dineo had coped with the trauma of it all. He wondered how he had survived all this time on his own with so much buried inside. He decided to pay him another visit. On his way to Dineo's apartment he passed by a mobile phone shop. 'It's about time the old boy joined the digital revolution,' Sam said to himself as he entered the store.

Dineo responded to Sam's knock and opened the door to his apartment with a beaming smile, 'Come in my friend, how are you?'

'I am good Dineo. I was thinking, how about we go for an early dinner?' asked Sam. 'It's on me.'

'That would be very nice,' Dineo replied. 'Give me a moment to put on a jacket and lock up.'

They arrived at The Regency and the waiter took them to a table outside, it was a lovely spring evening in Brighton, a perfect night for fish and chips and some people watching. The sun was setting to their right, skies were ranging from fierce orange to yellow. The sea was calm and glistening as they chatted.

'How has life been for you in the UK?'

'I would say good really. Over the years most people have shown me kindness and accepted me for myself. I have to say that I feel welcome here.'

'Life must have been so difficult for you in South Africa?'

'I wasn't in a position to judge in those days, I had nothing to compare it to. Looking back, I can see how oppressive things were. It was normal to be subservient and secondary.'

'Adjusting to life here must have been strange for you?'

'It was, learning to live and mix with people from other cultures has been a massive transformation for me.'

Dinner arrived and Sam waited until the waiter moved off, 'Do you mind if we talk about the massacre Dineo?'

Dineo looked at Sam for a second and replied, 'I think that will be okay.'

'So, going back to the incident Dineo, how much did you know about it?'

'Nothing, other than being attacked.'

'So you have no idea why you were targeted at the bus station that day?'

'No, I have no idea. Do you know?'

'It took a while for the story to come out back then, but yes, I do.'

Sam proceeded to inform Dineo of what had happened at the school, how Amy had been killed by a truck driver. How the truck driver had fled from the scene. The massacre was an act of revenge for the death of the child.

Dineo nodded his head, 'I guessed that it was some form of revenge. The whites dishing out some of their justice to the black man.'

'When you were questioned by MI6, did they know of the massacre Dineo?'

'If they did, they did not discuss it with me.'

Sam told Dineo that the final body count for the massacre was around 32. The killers were never caught and that it was only a short time before it was no longer news or even a discussion point in the white community.

'One thing I don't get Dineo, why did you run so far? Surely just getting away from the gunfire would have been enough?'

Dineo leaned forward and spoke softly to Sam, 'I knew one of the killers, he saw me at close quarters. I had to get far away, he would never have let me live.'

'And did you tell the UK authorities that?'

'No way, I thought they may have sent me back to South Africa if I had. You are the first person I have told of this.'

Sam felt both shocked and privileged, 'You have kept this to yourself all these years Dineo, so who was this person?'

'His name was Jaap Van NieKirk. He was the son of a farmer that I once worked for, before I started the driving job. His parents thought he was an angel, but I knew different.'

'Enlighten me, please.'

'He was evil. When his parents would go away for weekends or holidays, Jaap's behaviour would change dramatically. He would have his friends come around to the homestead. There was always drug smoking and girls involved. They all thought we farm workers were blind and stupid, but we knew what was going on.'

Sam felt for Dineo. He gave him a reassuring smile, 'Carry on my friend.'

Dineo continued, 'One day, one of the farm workers got a little too close to what was going on in one of the barns. I witnessed him being dragged off by Jaap and another white man. They threw him in the back of a Bakkie and headed for the dirt track leading down to the Kraal, that was the last we seen of that worker.'

'What do you think happened to him?'

'The next day I was working near the Kraal. They had done a good job of cleaning up after them but there was enough evidence of blood and skin on some of the rocks lying between the tire tracks that had been made in the dirt. They must have dragged him behind the Bakkie and dumped his body somewhere.'

'Dumped?' asked Sam.

'Yes, there were plenty of old mine shafts around the place, he would never ever be found in one of those.'

'Surely someone would have missed the worker and said something?'

Dineo just looked back at Sam with half a smile, 'When Jaap's father returned, he lined us all up in the morning before we started work and told us that that farm worker was no longer employed. Apparently Jaap had reported him to his father for stealing and he had been sacked.'

'And that was the end of it Dineo?'

'As far as Jaap's father was concerned, yes. But Jaap had his way of reminding us to keep quiet.'

Sam grinned, 'Yes I bet he did, go on.'

'As we were working, he would drive alongside us in his Bakkie. He would get out and lean into the back and pick up the end of a coil of rope and tie a knot in it. All the time smiling at us. Then he would get back in and drive off at speed.'

'Thank you for trusting me and opening up about this Dineo, Sam leaned over and touched Dineo on the shoulder. But you can't let him get away with these things.'

Dineo looked back at Sam, wondering how on earth he could do anything about this now. They finished dinner and Sam suggested a walk along the sea front. They talked more as they headed east along the promenade.

Sam turned to Dineo, 'Do you want justice my friend?'

'All of this was a long time ago. Even those people from MI6 told me that incidents like mine tend to be covered up. Their advice was to forget it and move on, make a new life.'

'But is your conscience clear Dineo? I get the impression that there has been no closure for you.'

'No, it is not clear, this never ends for me.'

They reached a bench that faced out to sea and Sam motioned for them to take a seat.

As Dineo sat down he said, 'It took me a long time before I was able to do this.'

Sam quizzed, 'Do what?'

'Sit alongside a white person on a bench like this.'

Sam's thoughts drifted back to what he had witnessed during his time in South Africa and nodded in acknowledgement.

'I have something to share with you now Dineo. My conscience troubled me for a long time over something that happened in my past and I needed help to move on to a better place.'

'Please Sam, tell me.'

'After I returned from South Africa, I joined the Marines. I thought I would enjoy the camaraderie like I did in the Merchant Navy. After a few years, I applied to join The Special Forces and I was accepted. A few more years and then the Balkans happened and I was whisked off to special operations in Bosnia.'

Dineo was engrossed in Sam's story.

'Officially the Brits were there to support the peace keeping activities. My mission was a little different, a much more discrete activity.'

'Doing what?' enquired Dineo.

'Mainly surveillance. We knew atrocities were occurring. It was our job to find out who were conducting them and how much of it was going on. We weren't meant to intervene, just witness and report back with the evidence that we gathered. It was inevitable that war crimes would be investigated later and we were helping build a case against the offenders.'

'But you did more than observe?'

Sam rolled his eyes to acknowledge Dineo's correct assumption, 'Serbian soldiers were running feral. Looting and raping. Indiscriminate killing of civilians was rife, all part of their ethnic cleansing. One afternoon I heard screams coming from a rural property as my unit came across it and I went to investigate. As I got close to the front of the house I saw the lifeless bodies of two kids lying outside. They must have been no older than six or seven. They had both been shot in the head.'

Dineo let out a sigh, 'Oh my lord.'

'It wasn't the first time I'd seen this, as I say, it was rife. I heard cries coming from inside the house. I knew from the cries what was happening to the poor mother of those kids. This time I couldn't stand by, so I went in. Two other Serb soldiers were watching the third one raping the woman. Maybe they had had their turn or they were waiting, I don't know. I took them out. As I did the third guy turned his head and looked up at me. Before I could fire a shot into him, he slashed the throat of the woman. Then I killed him. My unit had caught up with me by then. They moved off to clear the rest of the house and I pulled that bastard away from her. She was still alive, but mortally wounded. I held her hand and she squeezed mine until she bled out and passed away.'

'You are a brave man Sam.'

'Not really Dineo, I did the wrong thing.'

'Why? You killed the enemy and tried to save the woman.'

'There lies the problem, they weren't the enemy, we weren't meant to intervene. Only observe. Defending ourselves was only justifiable as a last resort.'

'What happened next?'

'Inquiry, jail, and I eventually got booted out of the Marines. My misdemeanour was dealt with internally.'

'Covered up?' asked Dineo.

Sam nodded, 'Yes you may call it that. Special operations have ways of managing those situations. I paid the price though.'

'And you suffered with your conscience you say?'

'I took three lives in a fit of anger.'

'You avenged that innocent family Sam.'

'I crossed the line, it wasn't my place to play God.'

'So what was next for you?'

'I was out and on my own. I struggled to make sense of it all. I blamed myself for letting my emotions get me into that mess. I travelled around the world for a couple of years, just drifting, drinking, fighting. I eventually met a lovely American lady when I was on a holiday in Florida Keys. She helped me get through it.'

'Were you a couple?'

'Yes, but only for a while. We both had issues, demons we were running from. They say people come into your life for a reason, season or a lifetime. In this case it was definitely for a reason. She gave me the closure I needed to move on, to get my life back in order.'

'That is good Sam.'

'So Dineo, how do we get you the closure you deserve?'

'I don't know, what is your advice?'

'I think we need to find your demon and maybe we should go face him.'

Dineo opened his eyes wide with horror and said, 'And kill him?'

Sam laughed, 'I don't know if we should go that far, but facing him down will be a start my friend.'

'Where do we begin Sam?'

'How about you and I travel back to South Africa together and find him?'

'Then what?'

'Don't worry, we will think of the best way to deal with him. Things have changed so much in your old country.'

'But what about me, I may get into trouble. I have a good life here now, I don't want to jeopardise that in any way,' said Dineo looking worried.

'Leave it to me my friend, nobody will know we are there, trust me.' Sam laughed as he tapped his forefinger against his temple.

'I don't understand why you are getting so involved Sam, in fairness you hardly know me.'

'On the contrary Dineo, I believe I do know you and it's something I would like to be involved in.'

CHAPTER TEN

۞

Narrogin, Spring 2005

At first Lana would write to Jaap's mum Anneline every week. After six months when she began to feel more settled, this became once a month. It was expensive to call, so hand written letters were the preferred method of contact. Anneline was really good at keeping in touch, in fact she had been a wonderful mother in law overall.

Lana wrote:

Dear Anneline and Henny

So lovely to hear from you as always. Glad to hear that things are going well for you both.

It's hard to believe that it's been eight years since we left South Africa. Time just flies by.

Jaap sends his love. He has so many business interests now that it's hard to keep up with what he is doing. So many business trips, he travels all over Australia now. He has hired a farm manager to take care of the day to day running of things here.

It's proved to be a great decision as I can concentrate solely on my Tea Rooms.

The rooms are going so well. We are a regular stop off point for many of the bus tours that travel through Narrogin.

Andre will finish at high school this year. You would be so proud of him. Unfortunately, he is not so keen on pursuing a career in farming. He is so into Information Technology and is planning to take a Diploma in the subject. As you can imagine this has not landed well with Jaap. Sorry to say but they are often at cross purposes at just about everything nowadays. I pray that this is just a phase that Andre is going through. Jaap blames the company that Andre keeps for his attitude.

Have you guys changed your minds about getting a computer? It is a marvellous way to keep in touch. Email is such a wonderful thing and there is something called Skype now, you can make calls and even see each other on video. Andre uses it all the time, he's such a whizz with all those things. I know you said you are too old to be learning all that stuff but please think about it.

It would be so wonderful if you both could visit us here, but I fully understand your situation and how hard it would be for you to leave the farm for so long.

Ok, I am going to keep this short and sweet and get this off in the post to you.

Lots of love from us all

Lana, Jaap and Andre

Not everything that Lana wrote in her letters was strictly true. Jaap didn't send his love, at least he never communicated that to her. He rarely spoke of his parents and, if he had anything to say about them, he was critical of how they had distanced themselves from him.

Andre was doing well, as were the Tea Rooms. In fact, last year Lana and her business partner had moved to new premises. Much larger in size. She also omitted things from her letters. Like the fact that she and Jaap saw little of each other and when they did, he would be chastising her for being neglectful in looking after and caring for him. He appeared to be jealous of her success and her friends. Any time he got angry about something he would blame her and say she had caused it. He was always the victim. It was better she kept these things to herself. Jaap would go crazy if he ever found out that she had told his parents about those things.

―⁓―

Marcus was a lovely man. A travelling salesman who sold farming machinery, tractors, combines and related accessories. He had been coming into the Tea Rooms for more than six months now. He would stay for at least an hour, always having the same thing, cream tea. He was always polite and he had a nice smile.

'I think that man has a little thing for you Lana,' said Lana's business partner Karen.

Lana laughed, 'Karen, you are funny.'

'I am serious Lana.'

Lana turned to look at him and he looked up and smiled at her.

'Oh my goodness, do you think so?'

'I know so, he hardly takes his eyes off you. It's been like that for ages.'

Marcus sensed that the women were talking about him and pretended to read the menu.

Lana was a little embarrassed, but quietly excited by the attention. He was an attractive man and Karen had said that he had kind eyes. She couldn't help feeling a little disappointed when he settled his bill with Karen and did not say his usual farewell to her. Perhaps they had embarrassed him. Secretly, Lana hoped he would still keep visiting.

—◦—

Jaap was travelling more and more, he had little option. The Croatians had been calling all the shots since he had compromised himself with them. They used him and his skills to expand into new markets across Australia. He had long since given up about thinking of revenge. Instead he recruited new victims to administer his narcissistic meanness to. New supply was easy to find, whether it be people that worked for him or his many girlfriends that he shacked up with on his business trips to Melbourne, Brisbane, Sydney and Cairns.

He still raged at the Croatians and what they had done to him, but new supply definitely helped. He was raking in lots of cash, which always bought the adoration he craved.

—◦—

'Lana, you are wearing a bit more make up these days dear,' said Karen.

'Oh, why not?'

'It suits you love, I am sure Marcus will be impressed when he sees you'.

Lana laughed, 'If he ever comes back.'

As it happened, they didn't have to wait long, it was the following day that the salesman called into the Tea Rooms.

'Go on love, you take his order,' said Karen.

'Hello sir, nice to see you back, the usual for you?' Lana put on her best smile as she asked him.

'I need to ask something first. Can I be so bold to ask you to join me for a drink this evening?'

'I would love to say yes. But I am married and this is a small town,' replied Lana trying to show her disappointment without being too obvious.

'I am sorry, I didn't know for sure. The ring doesn't always mean the marriage is current.'

Lana was regretting her response already. She was so thrilled he had asked her out, she felt light headed. He motioned to stand up and leave and Lana said, 'Please don't go. Your cream tea is on us today.'

Lana headed to the kitchen area where Karen was waiting to talk to her. So?'

'I chickened out Karen. I had to tell him I was married.'

'Don't be such an idiot Lana. You are entitled to some happiness.'

Lana stared back at her, trying to figure out how Karen knew she was not happy.

'You don't have to say anything Lana. I have known you long enough to understand what kind of man your husband is. I ditched the bastard I was married to because he was the same as yours.'

Lana was shocked, how could Karen know this?

'He clearly has a personality disorder Lana. Once you have been a victim of it and finally admitted that you are, it's so easy to spot.'

Lana wanted to cry.

'We can talk about that later. But live in this moment, which is what I recommend you do. Take him to my place. Nobody will know. Just talk to him, you deserve to. He is a good man, I can tell. Trust me. Tell him you only want to talk. Find out if he has genuine feelings for you.'

'I have promised him cream tea.'

'Well bloody well take it with you. Silly cow.'

Lana walked over to Marcus and said, 'I think we need to talk, just talk.'

He beamed a smile back at her. Karen was correct, he did have kind eyes. Unlike the cold vacant pools belonging to her husband.

She gave him a slip of paper and said, 'Meet me there in twenty minutes.'

He took the paper, looked at the address and said, 'Thank you.'

Karen lived in a small duplex home in a quiet location a few minutes' walk from the Tea Rooms. Lana headed off and readied herself for the arrival of Marcus. She was very nervous and was not sure she was doing the right thing. But she knew she had to, she had to understand why she was feeling the way she did and if he felt that way too. She had sacrificed everything for Jaap. Was there something left in life for her?

The knock came on the front door. Lana opened it and ushered Marcus in quickly.

'Please, come through,' she said as she walked through to the open plan living and kitchen space.

They sat on chairs opposite each other and said nothing for what seemed like an age.

Then they smiled at each other at the same time.

Marcus said, 'Are we sixteen?'

That brought on a burst of laughter from them and eased the tension they were both feeling.

They both went to say something at precisely the same time and laughed again.

'You first,' offered Lana.

Marcus began, 'I just want to know if I am the only one feeling the spark.'

Lana smiled at him, 'No, no you are not alone there.'

'So now I do feel like a sixteen year old,' replied Marcus.'

'Me too.'

Lana felt exhausted, her emotions were roller coasting, 'I need some time Marcus.'

'You know my name?'

'It's on your credit card.'

'There's a touch of the bloody Sherlock Holmes about you Lana.'

'And you know mine,' Lana laughed.

'Well you and Karen have a habit of referring to each other with your first names, not a great mystery really. Yes, we do need time. You're in a marriage and I respect that.'

'And you?'

'I am a widower. I've been on my own since I lost my dear wife five years ago.'

Lana liked that response for two reasons, one being the fact he was single and the second reason was the obvious respect he still had for his late wife.

'I am glad we had this talk,' said Lana as she stood up.

Marcus stood and held Lana's left hand in his, 'Me too.'

As Marcus walked to the front door, Lana said, 'Oh, I brought your cream tea here, you haven't had it.'

'You know Lana, I have never really liked cream teas. Maybe I can try something else when I visit next week.'

'I am sure we will find something to suit your taste,' said Lana with a broad smile on her face.

☙

Chapter Eleven

Brighton April 22nd, 2018

It was a rainy Sunday morning. More like drizzle really. Sam had arranged to meet Dineo in the foyer of the Grand Hotel at 10 am. He was already waiting when Sam arrived.

'I hope you've not had breakfast. I've booked us a table in the Victoria Terrace. The brunches are great there.'

'You're very kind Sam. I've not eaten yet, that'll be perfect. Thank you.'

'My pleasure.'

The waiter led them through to their table for two by the windows looking out onto the seafront.

'It's amazing how busy Brighton is, even when the weather is not so good, eh Dineo?'

Dineo looked out of the window and replied, 'I like this place, I always have. There's something about the light here, something uplifting.'

'I have a gift for you,' Sam slid the mobile phone over to Dineo. 'It's nothing fancy but you'll need it for what we are about to do.'

'Which is what exactly?'

'We're going to South Africa in a few weeks. We are going to find Jaap.'

'Oh, my Lord, you are a quick mover Sam,' said Dineo as he picked up the phone and inspected it.

Dineo was clearly shocked at the thought or returning to South Africa, but Sam detected a hint of a smile under the surprise. Sam rang the number for Dineo's new phone and Dineo almost dropped it as he fumbled with it in his hands.

'What do I do, I have never had one of these things?'

Sam reached over and pressed the red button on the screen, 'I can see I will have to give you some lessons, we'll get back to that later. Meanwhile let's order, I'm Hank Marvin.'

Dineo looked back at Sam really confused.

'It means, I'm starving, it's a kind of rhyming slang.'

'Oh,' Dineo simply replied.

'Never mind, I can throw in a few lessons for that as well,' Sam said with a grin.

When they had finished their brunch, Sam took out a laptop from his backpack.

He pulled his chair round to sit alongside Dineo and logged on.

'Now, let's have a look at where the farm is, the one you worked on belonging to the Van NieKirks.'

When google earth loaded, Sam entered Rustenburg as the destination. Dineo watched on with amazement as a graphic of the earth rotated and homed in on an aerial view of Rustenburg.

'How close to Rustenburg was this farm Dineo?'

'It was halfway to Magaliesburg, close to a place called 'Olifantsnek'.

Sam plotted directions from Rustenburg to Magaliesburg and a blue line appeared to display the route.
Then he used his fingers on the screen to zoom in on
the area around Olifantsnek. Dineo was in a new world
now.

'Okay Dineo, help me out here.'

Dineo moved his head as close to the screen as he
could and pointed at a dam.

'Ten minutes drive after that dam we would turn off
the road and onto the farm track.'

Sam calculated how far it would take to travel a
further ten minutes, moved along the screen to follow
the road and zoomed out slightly to look for a building
that could be a farm.

'Did you turn left or right off the road?'

'Travelling to the farm from Rustenburg, we would
turn left.'

Sam located what could be a homestead and zoomed
in as far as he could, then switched to street view mode.
'Is this the farm?'

Dineo sat back in his chair, his jaw dropped and he
nodded his head repeatedly, 'Yes, that is it.'

Sam watched him for a moment, observing the shock
that Dineo was obviously experiencing at catching up
with technology so rapidly.

'It looks just as it did. The road, the track up to the
farm, the mountains in the background. Can you find
the bus station in Rustenburg Sam?'

'I don't imagine it looks the same now Dineo, let me
try though. Was it the one next to Pick N Pay?'

Dineo nodded, 'Yes it was.'

Sam searched for Pick N Pay, Rustenburg, the
software reacted immediately and homed in on his

requested destination. He clicked the option for street view and Dineo looked on, amazed once again as he saw clear images of the building that happened to be the last thing he saw of Rustenburg prior to his escape. Much had changed, but the warehouse and loading bays looked much the same as they did 35 years ago.

Dineo let out a deep breath and moved his face right up to the screen as if he were about to climb into it, 'This is incredible Sam.'

'This technology will be a great help to us Dineo.'

Sam took as many details as he could from Dineo about the Van NieKirk family. After many hours of scanning through the most popular social media platforms, he drew a blank on any genuine leads. The family name was just too common. It looked like old fashioned leg work would be the order of the day.

Sam booked return flights to Johannesburg. They would be flying out on May 2nd. He tentatively booked a return date but with an option to change, that would depend largely on what they discovered.

✿

CHAPTER TWELVE

Narrogin Spring 2005 (Continued)

Karen was so excited to hear of how things had gone with Lana and Marcus. There was no way she would phone Lana at home, so she waited until the next morning until Lana came into the Tea Rooms.

'You don't have to bloody say a thing mate,' shouted Karen and she ran over and hugged the very happy looking Lana.

Lana couldn't stop smiling, 'He is so nice Karen. I don't know what to do. He has relit feelings that I thought were gone forever.'

Karen could see Lana had a tear in her eye and offered her a napkin from one of the tables. Lana took it and dabbed at her eyes.

'You can't bloody leave it there mate, come on spill the beans.'

Lana took a seat at one of the tables, 'We obviously have feelings for each other. I told him I need time. He is a widower and respectful of the fact that I am married.'

'We need to talk about your marriage Lana. Things are not good there, are they?'

Lana burst into tears, 'I have been thinking a lot about what you said. How did you know?'

'Let me ask you. Does he blame you for everything, treat you like dirt then pour admiration onto you as if nothing has happened? Does he rubbish all your friends and family? Does he have an unnatural interest in how he looks and appears to other people, especially new friends or business associates? Does he give you and others the silent treatment for long periods of time? Most importantly, does he have a lack of empathy for others?'

'My God Karen, stop please.'

'I am sorry hun, I didn't mean to...'

Lana cut her off, 'No sweetie. You are telling my life story. I haven't questioned this before. No, that's not true. I have, but I did not feel empowered to do anything about it. I thought all of this was just normal for married people.'

Karen sat alongside Lana and hugged her, 'Do you want to go home for the rest of the day? I can manage here today by myself honey.'

'No Karen, I will be fine thanks. I need to reflect and take this onboard. Here is the best place for me right now.'

'Okay, fair enough love.'

'So, what do I do Karen?'

'You do nothing for now. You need to fully understand Jaap's disorder first. Then you can look at your options love.'

'How do I find out about it?'

'Well, I am here. It's something I've been through and there is lots of help online too. Forums, YouTube and things like that. I warn you though, it's not going to be easy. You are married to a master manipulator. Plus, you don't want to let him know you are onto him.'

'Oh my, I've been such a fool,' said Lara raising her hands to cover her face.

Karen reacted angrily, 'No you bloody well have not. You have been his victim Lana. He has taken advantage of your sweet, honest and trusting nature.'

Lana looked helplessly at Karen, 'Karen, you know I have no one. I have no family of my own. I was orphaned as a child and have no Aunts, Uncles or cousins. Besides, even if I did, they would be miles away in South Africa. Andre and Jaap are all I have.'

'He knew what he was doing when he found you,' replied Karen.

'What does that mean?' asked Lana.

'Sorry love, there is much to learn. Slowly, slowly. Just let me help you. This is going to take time.'

───

Marcus never returned to the tea rooms again, well not in person anyway. He did post a letter through the door three weeks after his meeting with Lana. Karen picked it up off the floor and handed it to Lana.

Lana looked and Karen and said, 'If you don't mind, I am going to have a walk and read this alone.'

'Sure honey,' replied Karen.

Lana walked along the Main Street of Narrogin and found a bench seat outside the post office building. She sat and opened the letter.

Dearest Lana

As much as it pains me to write this, I feel it is the only option left open to me.

For thirty years I was privileged to share my life with a wonderful lady. I never once felt the need to seek the company of another woman.

After she was taken from me, I simply threw myself into my work, never thinking that there would be anyone else for me.

That was until I saw you. You have constantly been in my thoughts, day and night.

During my wife's illness she always told me, when the time came, to move on and enjoy life. I would always tell her that I was not interested, no one could ever replace her. That always brought a smile to her face, usually accompanied by a squeeze of my hand.

In her final days she would say to me, 'You have given me a wonderful life you old bugger. Don't think twice if you meet someone later that can bring you happiness, it's what I would want for you.'

As much as I believe that you and I could share something special, I cannot find it in myself to come between you and your husband.

So, for that reason, I think it is only fair that I refrain from contacting you again.

I am sorry that this cannot go any further as I would have loved for it to.

Farewell Lana
Your friend and admirer
Marcus Land

Lana read the letter three times and sat in silence as the town of Narrogin woke up around her. She carefully folded the letter and placed it back in the envelope.

Karen was standing outside the front door of the tea rooms awaiting Lana's return.

As Lana approached Karen asked, 'Well love, let me have it, good or bad?'

Lana handed the letter to Karen and, without comment, walked past her and into the Tea Rooms. Karen thought it best to say nothing and just read the letter by herself.

'Right, if the bastard thinks he is getting off the hook that easy he has another think coming,' she shouted to Lana as she entered the tea rooms and closed the shop door behind her.

Lana looked up from the table she was dressing and said, 'What do you mean?'

'Nice bloody letter and everything love, but it's bullshit if he thinks it's over between you two.'

Lana started to laugh, 'Oh Karen, what would I do without you?'

'Probably have a peaceful boring life mate,' Karen replied.

When they both stopped laughing Lana said, 'It's a nice thought, but I don't have any way to contact him. He didn't leave a number or an address.'

Karen pointed at her feet and then to her head and said, 'Down there for dancing, up here for thinking mate.' Then she walked over to the till and from a small box she took a business card and showed it to Lana. 'I took this from him a few weeks ago when I thought he was showing you too much interest, just in case,' she winked.

'What are you going to do Karen?

'I am going to phone the bugger.'

Lana felt uncomfortable and nervous. This was all happening too fast. There was no doubt she still loved Jaap. In spite of his ways, he was her man.

'No, Karen. Please not now. I have to get things right in my head first. I don't want to start something I can't continue with. It's maybe a good thing Marcus has backed off for now.'

Karen listened to her friend and empathised with her, 'Okay love, let's leave it for now.'

Jaap arrived back on the farm on the following Thursday evening. Lana was watching TV in the lounge. The lounge door opened and Jaap poked a huge bunch of flowers through the opening, then stuck his head through the door bearing a huge smile.

Lana could not help herself from smiling and feeling happy thoughts. They had not been speaking to each other for a couple of weeks. She instantly recalled how charming he could be.

The words, 'I'm sorry' we're not in Jaap's vocabulary, but he was adept at dancing around with other phrases that substituted the normal phrase used for an apology, always having the desired result. He sat on the sofa alongside Lana and handed her an envelope.

She immediately thought of the other envelope she had handled earlier in the week and instantly felt guilty.

He said, 'Go on then, open it.'

She opened it and took out the contents. She looked at the first class air tickets and hotel reservation for a four day stay at the Lizard Island Resort, Great Barrier Reef, Queensland.

'Oh my goodness Jaap. This is wonderful,' she said with a voice trembling with emotion.

'Nothing is too wonderful for my wife,' he replied and kissed her passionately.

Discard over, he had hoovered her back in with an expensive love bomb.

'You must call Karen and ask her to get some help this weekend Lana, you have been working so hard. You need, no, we need this break together.'

Lana was ecstatic, was this what she had been waiting for? Love back in her marriage. Things had been so bad for so long, it felt so good to have hope back again.

Karen was really trying to help, but she wasn't married to Jaap. How could she compare her ex with him? Besides, Karen had a habit of putting words in other people's mouths, Jaap had always said that.

Lana called her friend and business associate straight away, 'Karen, I have some good news and some bad news.'

'Oh, evening hun, let me have it then.'

'I am going to Lizard Island Resort for a weekend. Bad news is, it's this weekend,' said Lana. Then she waited for the response.

'Is your hubby there?'

'Yep.'

'And are you going away together?'

Lana felt awkward after the conversations they had held about Jaap earlier, 'Yes.'

Karen knew exactly what was happening. Now was not the time to intervene.

'Don't you worry about the cover, I will bring in the Saturday girl. Have a lovely time honey, you deserve a break. Send me a postcard for the notice board in the Tea Rooms.'

Lana was relieved that the call went okay, 'Thanks so much Karen. See you when I get back next week.'

As Lana ended the call, Jaap asked 'All good?'

'All good,' replied Lana.

Jaap held out his hand, 'Let's have an early night honey.'

It had been seven months since the wonderful weekend at Lizard Island Resort.

'But mum, I can't continue living here, that bastard is driving me crazy,' screamed Andre.

'Andre, language please.'

'Sorry mum, but I am not his possession. He is an absolute control freak.'

Karen's words were ringing in Lana's ears, but she pleaded with Andre 'He means well Andre, he would love you to carry on the farming tradition for the family.'

'That would not make him any less of a control freak if I did. He is bloody obsessive,' Andre responded angrily.

'Calm down Andre. Where would you go if you left and what would you do?'

'Guy and Glen are going to rent a house in Perth, there is a room for me if I want to join them.'

'And what are you going to live on?'

'I have secured a place at college studying Information Technology and I will get a part time job and a loan if I have to. But I am not staying here.'

Lana knew it was his dream to work with computers, 'Let me talk to your father.'

'No, no, no,' Andre reacted furiously. 'You may not see it mum, but he treats you like kak most of the time. If I stay here, I may do something I regret.'

Andre stormed out of the homestead and left Lana to reflect on his words.

In truth, Lana knew this was coming. Jaap was blowing hot and cold with her, blaming her for the breakdown of his relationship with his son. He was also constantly on Andre's case for anything and everything, mainly via text messages and emails, as he was away most of the time.

In truth, the good period with Jaap only lasted a couple of weeks after Lizard Island. It took a bit of humble pie eating but when Lana raised her issues with Karen, her friend stepped up without so much as a ' I told you so'.

Lana waited until there was a short break of service in the tea rooms, 'Andre wants to leave home Karen.'

'That's not good news for you Lana, he is the reason you are hanging on to your sanity mate.'

Lana smiled, 'I know. But I don't want to hold him back.'

'Then let him go, but you need to have a coping strategy for yourself if you do.'

Lana knew her friend was right. She was finally accepting that Jaap had a personality disorder that wasn't going away.

'I am sorry I didn't listen to you Karen,' she said sheepishly.

'There's nothing to apologise for Lana. There's nothing better than self-realisation to motivate you to change things. Have you reached that point love?'

'When my son leaves the farm, I am out of there too,' Lana's eyes were full of tears but she was displaying a strength that Karen had not seen before.

'Good on ya girl,' replied Karen as she hugged Lana. 'Promise me, if doubts start creeping back in, just remember, he is unfixable.'

✿

CHAPTER THIRTEEN

Western Australia July 2010

By now the Australian Van NieKirks were largely living separate lives. Andre had moved to Perth and was sharing a house in the trendy suburb of Subiaco with two of his Aussie mates. He graduated with his Diploma in 2009 and found a job straight away. He had maintained no contact with his father since the day he left the farm. He loved his mum and still had a good relationship with her, albeit a distant one.

One month after Andre moved out, Lana left the farm and moved in with Karen for a short while. Karen was Lana's rock, helping her each step of the way to begin a new life.

'No contact means no contact Lana. Block his calls and messages and if he turns up here, or at work, you must say nothing to him. Walk away, do not respond.'

Karen was Narrogin born and bred, she had friends in high places in the town and used whatever means she could to help protect Lana. They knew when Jaap was in town and, with the help of the local Police Sergeant, were able to monitor his comings and goings. Jaap's vehicle received a fair amount of police attention, as did his sobriety whilst he was behind the wheel.

If Jaap was not the flavour of the month then there was no way he would be hanging around. Besides, he had charmed his way in with the Croatian Mafia in Melbourne and had established himself as a key figure in organised crime across Australia. He found it so amusing that his introduction to the Melbourne Croatians by the Fremantle Croatians would be their biggest mistake. They had given him free rein to impress the more senior Mafia figures and pave the way to lord himself over them.

International laws on money laundering had tightened up massively since 2001, but as his usual reimbursement was largely made in hard currency, this was not really a problem for him. With safe deposit boxes in several major banks in all State capitals across Australia, he was able to maintain his charmed secret life.

—m—

Australia. 28th September 2013

It was Aussie Rules Grand Final day. This being one of the biggest events in Australia and the ultimate prize in Australian Rules Football for the victor. The city of Melbourne was a buzz. Bars, clubs and homes all over Australia were getting ready for the match. 100,000 attendees would be present at the MCG to watch the Fremantle Dockers take on Hawthorn, nicknamed 'The Hawks'.

Twenty six year old Andre was living the dream. He was pursuing his career of choice and had achieved great things. He had rapidly advanced to the position of Senior IT Manager for one of the biggest mining and mineral companies in Western Australia. He worked from a prestigious office block situated on St. Georges Terrace in Perth's Central Business District.

He and his mates had planned a big day that would begin with a champagne breakfast and a barbecue in Kings Park, enjoying the stunning views of the city and the Swan River. Then it would be back to the house in Subiaco to watch the game on a big screen in the garden.

Bounce down, the equivalent of a kick off in soccer, was due at 2:30pm Australian EST. Andre was as happy as a pig in the proverbial, great job, great mates, ice cold beer on tap and the best seat in the house to watch the Grand Final. Could life get any better?

As the game reached the halfway point or the end of the second quarter as it is termed, the TV cameras were scanning around the MCG capturing shots of the adoring fans.

'Geez mate, isn't that your old man?' shouted Guy as he pointed to a close up shot of a man in one of the hospitality boxes.

Andre looked at the screen just as the image faded into another shot of a kid in the front row of a stand in another part of the ground, 'Couldn't give a shit if it was mate, arsehole that he is anyway.'

Guy and Andre laughed raucously and simultaneously shouted, 'Come on you Dockers,' and clashed their stubbies together.

Andre watched the rest of the game but couldn't help thinking of whether it was his father or not, it kind of disturbed him that it may have been. The post match party went on late, until the neighbours complained about the noise and it finished up at about 1am.

'Let's go have a look and see if it was the old bastard,' Andre suggested to Guy.

They walked into the lounge and rewound the recording of the game until they reached the spot in question, then froze the shot on the TV screen.

'I would say that is the prick,' slurred Andre.

'Yeh and look who he's with.'

'Who?'

'That's Goran bloody Bosnic mate, he's one of the owners of the night club in Freo. Bit of a bad egg that one mate,' said Guy.

'Yeh?'

'If your old man is keeping company with him Andre, he is up to no fucking good mate.'

Andre was indifferent, he had no love for his father and really did not care what he was up to as long as he stayed away from him and his mum.

༖

CHAPTER FOURTEEN

South Africa. May 2018

Dineo was excited and frightened. Sam had warned him that things would be very different to how he had known them. Apartheid was long gone, but there was a level of crime and disorder present now that had never been known in the country. Carjacking, rape and murder were rife and part of everyday life across all racial groups in today's South Africa. Levels of poverty, if anything, were worse now. Sam did not show Dineo any videos or social media streams that highlighted how bad things were, it was his job to shelter and protect his friend while they visited his old country. Their goal was to find closure and maybe some justice too.

The announcements on the South African Airways flight were made in both English and Afrikaans. Although it was the first time Dineo had heard Afrikaans spoken in many years, he was amazed at how fluent he still was. Although it was not his mother tongue, it gave him a warm feeling to hear it again. He began to feel more excited about what was waiting for him. They had taken an overnight flight, and as the cabin lights went down, they drifted off to sleep for a few hours. They landed in Johannesburg at 8am.

Sam picked up the hire car on arrival and plotted the route to Olifantsnek into the GPS. A visit to the Van NieKirks farm would be the first priority. The journey would take about two hours. They approached the Magaliesberg mountain range from the south and the view was stunning. Sam was no longer the young man in a hurry and he took the time to appreciate the natural beauty that was unfolding in front of him. For a moment he saw himself travelling on this same road in a minibus at the other end of his life and he smiled to himself. Dineo had been drifting in and out of sleep for much of the car journey so far.

'Okay Dineo, I need you to look out to the right and pick up the turn off to the farm, I would say it will be coming up in the next few minutes.'

Three minutes later and Dineo was in familiar territory, 'Slow down Sam, it's coming up now.'

Sam turned off the tar road and onto the red dust track as directed by Dineo.

About 1 km up the track they reached a gate, Sam stopped and Dineo got out of the car. As he approached he saw the police tape hanging from the gate posts. It was the first indication that something was not right. Dineo pulled the old steel tubular gate open and Sam passed through. Dineo slid back into the passenger seat, 'Something has happened here, be careful Sam.'

As the homestead came into sight, fronted by a row of Jacaranda trees, they passed a wooden sign displaying the words, 'WELKOM BY ONS HUIS'.

More police tape, this time across the front door of the property.

Sam pulled up under the shade of the jacarandas and listened for a while to ensure they were not being followed, 'This doesn't look good.'

As they approached the homestead they could see that one of the front windows was smashed, but the steel security bars were still intact. Sam moved over to look through the windows, 'Best look from here first Dineo.'

The sun was shining in from a side window providing enough light to see clearly into the main living and dining room. An old dining table took centre place. They tried the front door, it was locked.

'There is an entrance at the side' Dineo offered. 'Follow me.'

More police tape, but the side entrance door was hanging on its lower hinge. There was enough space for Sam and Dineo to get through and into the property. From the stale stench it was clear that the place had been uninhabited for a while, however, a lot of personal items were still there.

Sam shouted from the outside, 'Hello, anyone here?'

No response came back. They crossed the threshold of the house and worked their way through the utility area, cautiously proceeding down the central passage way and into the main living and dining area. The room looked as if the owners may still be around, but it was soon clear they were not. In the centre of the dining table stood a wooden cross with a plaque alongside it. The plaque bore some hand scribed Afrikaans words.

Sam stooped to read it, 'What does this say Dineo?'

Dineo translated it, 'To our beloved friends. Henny & Anneline. May you rest in peace with God.'

'Is that the farmer you worked for Dineo?' asked Sam.

Dineo picked up an old family photograph that was perched on a sideboard and handed it to Sam and replied, 'Yes, this was them.'

'What happened here?' Sam questioned openly as he stepped from the main living room and back into the passageway, 'Let's check the other rooms.'

They opened the door to the master bedroom. What greeted them confirmed what Sam was already thinking to himself. The chalk silhouettes of where the bodies had lain were still visible on the floor at the entrance to the bathroom. Some heavy blood stains were present on the wooden flooring at the position of where the knees and feet of both victims would have been.

'It's a farm robbery and murder Dineo. It's happening so often nowadays.'

Dineo looked saddened by the discovery, 'They did not deserve this, they were old school Afrikaners, but these folks were not bad people Sam.'

Sam and Dineo walked through the remaining rooms of the homestead, it was clear that someone had tended the place after the police had concluded their business.

'I don't think this happened that long ago,' Sam declared.

Items had been neatly stacked in each room, as if ready for a pick up later. Several shoe boxes had been placed on the table in the kitchen area. Sam took a seat at the table and removed the lids of the boxes to view their contents.

Dineo was looking at some postcards stuck on the fridge door, they were from Australia, mainly from Perth, but there was also one from Lizard Island in

Queensland. There was a photograph placed just below that card. Dineo took it off and looked closely at it. He placed it in front of Sam and pointed to the young man on it. 'That is Jaap Van NieKirk.'

'The gunman?'

'Yes. What did you find in those shoe boxes Sam?'

'Nothing yet, come look with me.'

They began looking through the boxes in turn. Most of them were bills and formal letters with some old family photos amongst them. Sam stood up and checked a cupboard above the sink and found a plastic container. It was full of letters, airmail letters from Australia. Sam picked out the letter on the top of the pile and looked at the sender's name and address on the rear of the envelope and handed it over to Dineo, 'Look who this is from.'

Dineo read out loud, ' Mev. L van Nie Kirk, 13 McKay Way, Mandurah, WA 6230.'

'I think we have seen all we need to Dineo. Let's take these letters and that photo of young Jaap.'

They left via the door they came in. Dineo walked around the back of the homestead and Sam followed him, 'Where are you going?'

'I just want to check this area out for old times' sake, if that's okay?'

Sam replied, 'Yes, of course.'

Dineo took the photo of Jaap and lifted it up so it appeared to blend in with the background. Sam watched on. It looked like Dineo was trying to recapture a moment in time.

'You okay Dineo?'

Dineo turned around to face him and smiled, 'Thirty five years Sam, where did it go?'

They made their way back to the car and Dineo asked, 'Do you think Jaap and his family know about the murder?'

'I really don't know Dineo, that's gonna be a hard one to qualify,' Sam thought for a moment. 'We could try the neighbours. Then again, we don't want to give the game away to Jaap. Let's go through these letters first.'

Sam listened for a while before getting back into the car and driving off. He didn't want to encounter anyone while he was on the property. As they made their way back to the main tar road, the red dust was whipping up and they could taste it as it bellowed in through the open windows. Dineo watched the homestead disappear from view through the passenger side wing mirror. He was reflecting on what he had seen and how ironic it was that the parents of Jaap had suffered such a terrible end to a lifetime spent on their beloved land. Sam had explained what the staining on the wooden floor signified. Torture was a common means to extract information from the old vulnerable farmers and the drill was the preferred tool of choice.

'Where to now Sam?'

'I have booked us a night at a motel on the outskirts of Rustenburg. We can think our next moves this evening over a cold beer.'

'Sounds like a plan to me man,' said Dineo.

It was still a little too early for them to check into the motel, so they parked up the car and took out the letters. Everything was written in Afrikaans. All of the letters were addressed to Jaap's mother and she must have kept them all. They dated back to 1997 and the last one was posted in Mandurah, Australia, on the 12th March 2018.

Sam held it up and showed it to Dineo, 'This one may reveal a lot to us.'

'How's your Afrikaans my friend?' he asked Dineo.

'I think it's still okay.'

'Let's see,' Sam said as he opened the envelope and laid the pages flat on his knee.

He took out his phone and scanned each page using a language translator app. Once again Dineo was mesmerised.

'Okay, you read the letter and we will confer once we have finished.'

Dineo took the hard copy and Sam commenced reading the digital translation.

Dear Anneline

I am very saddened that I have not heard from you in three months. I truly thought that in spite of my divorce from Jaap that we could still be friends.

You seemed to be ok with things while we were separated but maybe the divorce has made you think differently about things. Perhaps it was too much to expect that things could carry on as before. If that is the case please know that I do understand.

Andre is doing so well for himself. I know I have been the main communicator over the years as he and Jaap were happy to leave that to me. But going forward it may be better that you contact Andre directly. Here is his address:

<u>26 Geraldton Heights</u>
<u>Subiaco</u>
<u>WA 6008</u>

I am sure he would love to hear from you.
There will always be a special place in my
heart for you and Henny.

Love to you both

Lana

They finished reading within a few seconds of each other.

Sam now knew the first names of Jaap's parents, 'I am going to check on the Internet for farm murders over the past three months in this area, Dineo. There must be something online.'

He searched for a while but nothing of any substance came up.

'What was the name of the farm Dineo?'

'Berguitsig'

Sam opened the YouTube app and typed the name of the farm into the search box. It led him to a video. 'This could be interesting,' he said as he moved the phone so they could both watch the video.

The first minute of the video was all about the amount of farm murders that were occurring and how the targets were typically elderly and in isolated locations. Then it mentioned the Van NieKirk's and how they had been tortured and killed on their farm on the 15th March 2018. It showed some images of the homestead, first a shot from outside and then some shots of the room where their bodies had lain. A picture of the elderly couple was shown, then it faded as a video interview began with a neighbour. The neighbour was paying tribute to the warm couple and how they had served the community for most of their lives. He continued to say that it was a travesty how these attacks were becoming more frequent and seemingly allowed to happen. The video then cut to an image of many white crosses on a hillside in a place known as Plaasmoorde.

Sam stopped the video, 'There we go Dineo. As we thought, this happened recently.'

They checked into the motel and agreed to rest up for a couple of hours. Then they would meet up and go through the rest of the letters.

—◆—

The majority of the correspondence from Lana was essentially no more than pleasantries. However, after four hours of sifting through the letters, Sam and Dineo were able to track how things had unfolded for the Australian based Van NieKirk's following their emigration in 1997.

Sam could not help laughing as he said, 'So Lana ditched Jaap and his son has disowned him.'

Dineo responded with a laugh too, 'Can't say I feel sorry for him.'

'And we know where Lana and Andre are living. Hopefully.' Sam said with fingers crossed.

'Jaap could literally be anywhere in Australia.'

Sam winked at Dineo, 'We'll find him.'

—◆—

Sam booked the return flights for the next day. He chose the overnighter back to London. It was pointless hanging around here any longer than they had to.

They needed to find somewhere to eat dinner. Sam went across to the reception and asked the staff member on duty if she could recommend anywhere.

'You are not from around here are you?'

'No, just visiting for a couple of days.'

'Then I recommend that you don't venture into town. It's not safe. There's a really nice place nearby on Kock Street. Would you like me to call ahead and book you a table?'

'That would be great thanks. Can you make it for 8pm in the name of Sam?'

'Sure.'

'How bad are things in town?'

'Very bad once it starts getting dark. Drugs, robbery, carjackings. Many criminals have settled in Rustenburg over the last few years. It's not the safe little haven of my parents' time.'

'That is sad to hear,' Sam replied with genuine sympathy.

He wondered if his friends Andy and Sue, were still living here. He was tempted to look them up and decided against it. Some things were best left alone.

The restaurant was only a few minutes drive away. Sam parked the car under a street light as close to the front door as he could.

As they sat at their table Sam said, 'We have a free day tomorrow Dineo. Is there anything you would like to do while we are here?'

Dineo thought for a moment and replied, 'I would like to visit the bus station.'

'No problem.'

'And there is a place I would like to see once more.'

'Oh, where might that be?'

'It's a place I used to go to when I was a young boy. It's close to the township that I grew up in.'

'Can you remember how to get there?'

'Yes Sam, I will never forget that.'

They headed back to the motel and retired to their rooms, making arrangements to meet at 8am the next morning for breakfast.

As Dineo opened the door to his room he called to Sam who was standing a couple of doors away, 'Thank you.'

Sam nodded and smiled back at his friend without saying anything.

Sam lay on his bed fully clothed. Curiosity was getting the better of him, he could not come back to Rustenburg without seeing how much it had changed, dangerous or not, he had to see for himself. He quietly exited his room and drove into town. He had done some research on the Internet, but there was no substitute for seeing things at first hand.

As he approached the CBD area, the town started to show itself in a very different light to the one he had known. He stopped and double checked that the doors and windows were all locked in his vehicle. He had insisted that he was given an unmarked hire car. The criminal elements loved the 'easy picking' advertising that obvious hire cars gave them.

The main drag in town was heavy with prostitutes and drug dealers, there was no need to go any further. He did a U-turn and headed back to the restaurant on Kock Street. He had noticed the place had a sit up bar and there were a few locals drinking there. The waitress recognised him as he walked back in, 'Was the food that good?' she said.

Sam laughed and pointed at an empty bar stool, 'A couple of nightcaps I think.'

'Be my guest.'

He pulled up a stool and sat next to a man that must have been close to his age.

The man turned to him, 'Howzit man.'

Sam responded, 'Good thanks, and you?'

The man offered his hand, 'Piet, pleased to meet you. What brings you to this hellhole of a place?'

Sam looked at the barman who was laughing at Piet.

Piet said, 'Don't worry about him man, he knows I mean the town, not the restaurant.'

They all laughed.

Sam signalled for the barman to pull a drink for Piet and asked for a Cane and Coke for himself.

Sam picked up with the conversation, 'Just passing through.'

'Believe me man, you wouldn't want to stop any longer that you have to.'

'That bad, eh?'

'It breaks my heart man, the bastards are running wild here. There is no law and order. I should have gone when I had the chance years ago.'

Sam said nothing, he wanted to let the guy vent.

'What bastard on earth rapes a three year old child then sets the kid on fire?'

It was if a ghost appeared from Sam's past. An image from the horrors of Bosnia flashed in his mind.

'They take this shit called nyaope, it's lethal man. There's a bunch of Nigerian crime lords running things, peddling that stuff to anyone. That crap is turning this place into a war zone.'

Sam waited for his opportunity, 'And the farm murders, what's happening there Piet?'

Piet stared at Sam without speaking. Sam looked back with a solemn face.

'I lost some good friends a few weeks ago. They were tortured and murdered for nothing man.'

'Sorry pal, I didn't mean to....'

Piet cut Sam off, 'No, it's okay boet, people need to know what's going on here.'

'What is happening?' enquired Sam.

'It's been going on for years. The bastards target the farmers, they torture, rob, rape and murder. It's happening all over this part of the country. Like I said, it happened to my friends. Poor folks were all alone.'

'That's sad Piet, do you mean they were all alone when they were attacked?'

'No, they had no one, no family around. We, their friends, buried them. They had given so much to this community over their lifetime. Now their land is going to waste. These bastards aren't just killing people, they are killing the food supplies, the future.'

Sam knew Piet was talking about the Van NieKirk's, he dug a little more, 'They had no family?'

'They had a son, he went off to Australia with his family years ago. Lucky bastard.'

'Did he come back for their funerals?'

'No, don't suppose he will be back either. Not to worry though, we folks will rally around here and secure the property.'

Sam looked at his watch, 'I must be going, got an early start in the morning. Good to meet you Piet. Sorry to hear things are so bad for you. Good luck pal.'

They shook hands and Sam headed back to the motel. It was a stroke of luck meeting Piet, then again, the white community was shrinking here and probably closer than they had ever been. Maybe it wasn't so much of a coincidence.

CHAPTER FIFTEEN

Sam found Dineo outside the front of the motel, he was sitting on a bench looking up at the surrounding hills and enjoying the warmth of the morning sun.

'Penny for your thoughts,' said Sam.

Dineo smiled, 'Strange thoughts Sam, very mixed.'

'Let's have breakfast. I thought we might take a look into town this morning, then out to the place you want to see.'

'That sounds fine to me.'

Sam made his confession about his venture out on the previous evening.

Dineo responded with laugh, 'I thought the temptation would be too much for you.'

'It was. I drove into town but there was no way I was hanging around, it's as bad as I've seen anywhere. Hopefully we can access areas we want to during daylight hours.'

Sam didn't reveal everything, he would update Dineo later of his conversation with Piet.

As they approached the Main Street in the town, it was evident that some sort or demonstration was going on. The mood was clearly volatile. Sam parked up within good viewing distance but made sure they were out of harm's way. They wound the front windows down to listen to the chanting of the protesters.

Dineo interpreted the Tswana for Sam, 'They are shouting, foreigners out, drug dealers out.'

'Let's not get caught up with this Dineo. Remind me, how do we get to the bus stop?'

'Turn around and take your next left.'

Sam swung the car into the 'Pick N Pay' supermarket car park, he knew he was close to where Dineo wanted to be, but looked over to him for further instructions.

'Keep going around to the right until you reach the end of the car park and stop there.'

Sam pulled up and cut the engine. Dineo hesitated for a moment and opened the door letting in the steadily increasing heat of the Transvaal mid morning. He got out and sat on the car bonnet on the driver's side. Sam joined him.

'What you thinking Dineo?'

'I see myself running away all those years ago. Wondering if I did the right thing?'

'You made the right call my friend.'

'Maybe so?'

'Don't doubt yourself, you were a victim. Have you ever thought that you survived and escaped for a reason?'

Dineo gave it a few seconds before asking, 'Sam, can we take a drive, out of this town and into the bushveld?'

'Good idea.'

Before they got back into the car and left this unsavoury part of their past behind them, Sam asked, 'How about we get some boerewors, a six pack and a disposable Braai? Lunch in the bushveld.'

'That would be a great thing to do.'

They took the main road, Highway 4 towards Gaborone and headed to a beauty spot at Kgaswane

Mountain Reserve. Sam lit the coals and dodged the smoke. The views from the elevated picnic spot were sensational. South Africans regularly use the term 'shame'. It has a meaning of its own and can be used in a wide variety of contexts. When Dineo looked out over Rustenburg and the surrounding countryside, he used it. On this instance it was a declaration of sadness, he felt genuine pity for what he had witnessed on this return to his country.

The smell of the Boerewors was licking the air around them and stirring their stomach juices. Sam cut up sections from the coil of the spicy sausage and they washed it down with the beers. Sam looked over at Dineo, he had rarely met anyone he respected as much as he did him. Bellies full and a few beers taken, they drifted off into a peaceful doze in the late afternoon in a place that was so contrasting to the unruly and highly charged town of Rustenburg. Time was pushing on now and they had one place left to visit before making their way back to the airport.

It took them 20 minutes to drive to the turn off for the old township where Dineo had grown up. It was still in the hours of daylight, but Sam knew that alone was no measure of safe passage in these parts. They were both on the lookout for anything untoward.

The old township, or settlement as it was also termed, was obviously still an over- populated slum. Nothing more than shacks made of corrugated sheeting and wood. They were driving off road now and Sam avoided getting too close to the edge of the township. He reduced to a crawl to minimise the amount of red dust being stirred up by their vehicle. It was best if they were not seen.

'Let me know when we are getting close to your special place Dineo.'

Dineo pointed, 'Over there by that tree, the one that looks like it's growing upside down.'

Sam drove towards the Baobab tree and stopped a couple of metres short of it. Dineo opened his door and walked to the tree, he beckoned Sam to join him.

'Well, are we in the right place?'

Dineo was beaming, 'This is my place Sam, this is my tree.'

'How do you know, it's not the only one out here?'

'If you stand with your back to it and look towards the setting sun you will see the top of a mountain. If you wait until the sun drops onto the mountain top it will give off a flash of light. The sun always reflects off something, the flash only lasts a second. As a child that light gave me hope, as I watched it would lift my spirits, it was my connection with this land.'

Sam pointed over to some red dust clouds coming off the road to their left, 'Tonight may not be the best time to hang around and see it again Dineo, best we head off I think.'

As they drove back towards Johannesburg and the airport, Sam told Dineo of his chat with Piet. Both were reflecting on the experiences and discoveries made over the last two days. Sam was drifting into thoughts of how innocent and naive he had been in those days, how much the country had changed, how the balance of power had shifted between the races and peoples. Dineo was dealing with the floods of memories bringing flash images to his mind.

It took them two hours to reach the airport, it was quite dark when they arrived. Things would be beginning to happen in the cities and towns around them, other demons would be coming out to play, making the most of the lawlessness and corruption that supported their treacherous behaviours.

CHAPTER SIXTEEN

❦

Australia April 2018

When Jaap heard news of the murder of his parents, his first and enduring reaction was self-pity. He absorbed and revelled in all the attention he was receiving from people around him. It was all about him. He had had little contact with them in the 21 years since he had left them. Word came to him from one of his contacts in his corrupt network that went all the way back to the Rustenburg Police Force. He thought about contacting Lana and Andre to let them know the news but decided against it. The longer it went without them knowing of his loss would add to their guilt for the way they had treated him.

The new woman in his life, Debbie, was so upset for him.

'Do you want to go home darling? I realise that you've missed the funerals, but it may help.'

'I think it would be too much for me. I loved them so much. It would be too painful,' he skilfully lied.

He took Debbie by the hand and walked over to the window of his penthouse apartment. The views of

Sydney Harbour were amongst the best possible from the ritzy Double Bay suburb. Debbie was 25 years his younger and as gullible as she was beautiful.

Sam continued, 'No honey, whatever they went through they are at rest now.'

'It must be so hard for you?'

Jaap turned to look at her and just nodded softly to acknowledge her recognition of his pain.

Marcus heard the knock at the door. 'Andre, how are .....,' he cut himself short as he could see something was not right.

'Where's mum?'

'Come in, she is upstairs,' Marcus said as he walked to the bottom of the staircase. 'Lana, Andre is here love.'

Marcus pointed to the sofa, 'Take a seat Andre, what's wrong mate?'

Andre just stared back, it was obvious he had been crying, 'I want mum to be here Marcus.'

'Can I get you a drink?'

'Tea would be great thanks.'

Lana arrived in a dressing gown with a towel wrapped around her head, having just taken her morning shower. 'Andre darling, how nice to see you,' she said as she crossed the room intending to hug him.

Andre did not move from the sofa, he looked over to Marcus for him to join them. Marcus took the hint and sat on the other sofa alongside Lana facing Andre.

'Honey what's wrong?' Lana reached across the coffee table to hold Andre's hand.

'It's Ouma and Oupa.'

Lana and Marcus waited apprehensively for what he was about to say next.

'They have been murdered.'

Lana closed her eyes and started hyperventilating. Marcus supported her, it was not the first time he had witnessed her having an anxiety attack.

Andre stood up and crossed over to be closer to his mum, 'I only found out by chance this morning.'

Lana began taking slow deep breaths as Marcus held her hands.

'How, how did you find out?' she asked her son.

'Facebook of all places,' he replied. 'One of my friends posted a link about farm murders and I clicked on it.'

'And it was definitely them?' asked Marcus.

Andre nodded his confirmation.

Lana reached out and wiped the tears from Andre's eyes, 'When did it happen?'

'About three weeks ago I believe.'

'Do you know what actually happened?'

'Not now mum. Can we talk about that later please?'

There was never an intention for Lana and Andre to grow apart from Henny and Anneline, it just happened. Like a huge majority of families that emigrate to start new lives in far off places, the contact becomes less and less as new friends and life in the moment become the drivers and steal time. Priorities and previous loyalties can easily shift without making any conscious decision for that to happen. Despite these things, the pain Lana and Andre felt was immense.

Lana touched Andre's arm, 'Stay tonight Andre, please?'

'Sure Mum,' he replied. 'How about that cup of tea, Marcus?'

Andre sent a text to his house mates, Guy and Glen. *'Sorry fellas won't be there tonight. staying with mum for a couple of days. she took the news really bad.'*

They both replied with a thumbs up emoji within a minute. They had been great friends to Andre over the years. Guy also worked in Information Technology and Glen was a high-flying salesman, regularly away from home.

—⁓—

Nine years had passed since Lana found the courage, with Karen's support, to walk away from her marriage. It had not been easy. She remained in Narrogin and lived with Karen for twelve months. In that first year, Jaap had done his utmost to demean Lana to anyone and everyone in Narrogin that would listen to him. He slammed her at every opportunity. "She was clearly to blame for the break up, ungrateful for everything he had done for her." He had been successful in his gas lighting to a degree, mostly due to his manipulative expertise that disguised itself as charm to the well meaning folks out there that lent him their ears.

Fortunately for Lana, Karen had explained every move he would make before he actually made it. This helped to keep Lana's self doubt to a minimum. Eventually, Jaap took the path of least resistance and looked for new supplies and, over the years, he enjoyed meeting several. Each time reducing his victims self esteem to zero, whilst inflating his to maximum and accumulating the adoration he craved to fill his void.

—⁓—

Karen was a superstar. On Lana's 45th birthday she arranged a surprise party with one very special surprise guest, Marcus, and he and Lana have remained together ever since. When Marcus retired in 2014, the happy couple moved to the beautiful coastal town of Mandurah. Karen was a regular visitor and loved their beachfront property, she even had her own bedroom in their loving home. Marcus described her as a 'bonza woman.' He loved the fact that she enjoyed beach fishing as much as he did. On many an occasion they would be up and out of the house before Lana had even stirred, only catching up with her around 10am, when they came back to collect cold beers to take back down to the beach with them.

—⁓—

Glen was so grateful for the help and opportunities that Jaap had put his way. They clearly looked out for each other and he didn't want to jeopardise their special bond. That alone was why he kept it from Andre.

He took the call from Jaap, 'Glen, how's it going?'

'Fine, Mr. V.'

'And you say they know about the murders now?'

'Yes, definitely. It took a while, but I eventually got the link to pop up on his Facebook page.'

'And how did they react?'

'Very bloody badly apparently.'

'Good. Thanks Glen. Keep in touch buddy.?'

'Definitely Mr V.'

'Great.'

CHAPTER SEVENTEEN

On their arrival back in the UK, Sam and Dineo took the train from Heathrow to Brighton via London Victoria. Two hours later they were saying their goodbyes at the top of Queens Road as they left the railway station.

'Give it a couple of days and I will call you Dineo,' Sam said as he shook hands with him.

Sam's apartment was a ten minute walk down the hill towards the seafront and off to the right, close to the main shopping area in town. He needed a couple of days to figure out how to best approach and conduct the necessary research for their forthcoming trip to Australia. It was around 10am when he arrived home. He had a shower, made a coffee and went to work. His first task was to go through all of Lana's letters and gather names, places and identify any events that would present leads.

Lana had written fondly and frequently of her friend Karen in Narrogin and their Tea Rooms. That sounded like a great place to start. He googled Narrogin Tea Rooms and there it was, third on the list. He opened the website and there was a link to Facebook.

Sam was not a fan of Facebook, but he had established a false identity a few years ago. It was the best way to snoop. He logged on and opened the link to the Tea Rooms.

Karen was obviously a super user. It was also clear that she was using the medium to promote her business and had also provided a link to her Twitter account. To borrow a mining term, he had struck the mother lode. He searched Karen's friends first, then her photo albums.

It took him no time at all to locate Lana and Andre. After filtering through the photos, he now knew what they looked like. He took screen shots of their images and started to build portfolios of them. Lana had a low level of security and he was able to establish a profile of her personal details very quickly.

'In a relationship with Marcus'. 'Lives in Mandurah, Western Australia.' 'Best friend, Karen.'

He clicked on Marcus' image.

'Retired.' 'In a relationship with Lana.' 'Lives in Mandurah.'

He went back to Lana's photos and clicked on the folder 'Braai Mandurah New Years Day 2018'. There was Karen and Lana, obviously all the worse for wear on white wine, waving their glasses in the air and generally having a ball.

Andre was next, he had high security on his account. He wouldn't be learning anything about him from his Facebook account. He tried Twitter and Instagram, again nothing. He searched for him on LinkedIn and he found Andre's profile. It was all very professional, no comments, likes or dislikes on anything that could be perceived as political or that drove a personal agenda. Andre, it appeared, was quite a balanced, private person, at least that is what his online persona purveyed.

Sam reserved the final search for Jaap. As he thought, nothing at all. Perhaps he was using a different name now? Then again, he doubted that. Sam had learned from his time in the Special Forces that the best place to hide was in plain sight. He browsed for another hour until he felt he had enough to draw up a strategy for how to proceed.

—〰—

Sam had two reasons to leave Dineo alone for a couple of days. The first being to give his older friend time to get over the travel, and the second was to give him time to settle with his thoughts. He had to be sure that Dineo wanted to pursue this further and of his own volition.

—〰—

Sam had the makings of a plan in place and it was time to reconnect with his friend. The combination of Dineo's polite, gentlemanly nature and his lack of mobile phone know how was a source of amusement to Sam, enough to make him giggle to himself before he placed a call to him.

He called Dineo's phone and as usual it rang out twice before Dineo answered, 'Hello, yes.'

'Dineo, how are you pal?'

'I am well thank you, and how are you Sam?'

'All good here, are you okay for a catch up in an hour or so?'

'Yes.'

'Meet me at Brighton Railway Station, say 10.30?'

'Okay Sam, see you then, bye.'

Sam liked the buzz in the railway station and the coffee seemed to taste better there.

As Dineo approached Sam's table Sam stood and held out his hand to greet him, 'Hello pal, I ordered you your usual, it's in a takeaway cup so it should still be warm. How are you feeling, are your over the trip?'

'I am feeling good. In fact, I have never felt better.'

'That's so good to hear.'

They relaxed and said nothing while they finished off their coffees. Dineo broke the silence after a few minutes, 'We have to find that man Sam.'

Sam acknowledged his friends decision with nothing more than a wink.

'So, I've been busy in the meantime,' Sam led on. 'I can't place Jaap anywhere, but we have plenty of other stuff to go on. Here's my thoughts.'

Dineo listened intently as Sam recounted his online discoveries and suggested the way forward.

'Our first port of call will be Narrogin to meet with Karen.'

'Why Karen?' asked Dineo.

'She is solid Dineo. Her online friends clearly adore her. She is also responsible for making Lana a happier person. She has to be our first point of contact.'

'So what do we do next?'

'We have to decide on a date to get out there. I would suggest the sooner the better. Are you up for that?'

'Let's do it Sam.'

Sam admired Dineo's spirit, he was pushing 68 but had more go about him than most of the zombified phone-addicted millennials that seemed to be every-where nowadays.

'Well in that case, let's target a trip in three weeks or so. Australia will be at the end of its autumn, so we won't have to contend with the mad heat so much.'

'You said you found nothing on Jaap. Do you think it will be hard to track him down?'

'I Don't know' was all Sam could offer in response.

—w—

It took Sam almost three weeks to get visit visas sorted and flights booked to ensure they would arrive in Australia in the first week in June. In the meantime, he was checking the Facebook accounts of his people of interest on a daily basis. They should all be carrying on with their lives as normal when he and Dineo arrive in Australia.

꧁

CHAPTER EIGHTEEN

Western Australia. June 2018

Sam was still pretty fit for his 58 years, but even so, he knew the jet lag would kick in and slow him down. He needed a clear head for what was about to come, so he factored in a couple of days of relaxation at the front end for them. Besides, he had noticed that Dineo had been slowing up a little lately.

Although they had decided that Narrogin would be their first place to visit, Sam picked a hotel in Mandurah for them. After all, nobody knew them and it would give them a perfect opportunity to snoop around without attracting any attention to themselves. It would be great to see where Lana and Marcus were living and how they spent their days.

He chose the hotel well. Easy access into the town and a short walk to the beach. The same beach that ran in front of Lana's place. There was no need for Dineo to join Sam's snooping mission, in fact it was better that he didn't.

Sam was an early riser and a walk along the beach with a coffee in hand was a great way to start his day. The wet sand was cold on the soles of his feet, but it still felt good. The light was fantastic at 7:30 am and, as he walked north on the beach, the sun was rising to his right. As he approached Lana's place, he turned to his right and walked over to some sand dunes that kissed the front of her garden fence. He carried on for another ten meters and settled into a vantage point that would allow him a clear view without being spotted by anyone. He lay down on the dunes and listened and watched as morning broke on the household.

Marcus appeared on the upstairs balcony with a cup in hand. After a few minutes, Lana joined Marcus and they sat chatting together for ten minutes or so before returning inside. Sam thought about getting up and moving off, then changed his mind. He didn't want to kill the moment. Waves were crashing on the shore, it was cool but not cold and the sun was casting a wonderful light over the Indian Ocean. He lay back and closed his eyes. He drifted off into a peaceful sleep and when he awoke there was Marcus, down on the shoreline to his left, casting his fishing line into the breakers.

Sam felt good, he had aligned reality with what he had picked up on social media. It was too early to connect with Marcus. Sam chose his moment to leave the beach, exiting from a path in the dunes and taking a route that would allow him to pass the rear part of Lana's house. He took a photograph of the two cars parked on her driveway and cast his eye over the neighbourhood. It looked like a fairly new development. A bit squeaky clean for his liking. He made his way back to the hotel and caught up with Dineo. They would check out of the hotel the next morning and make their way to the wheatbelt town where it had all started for the Van NieKirk's.

—⁓—

Sam took the southern option for their trip to Narrogin from Mandurah. The route took them through the Dwellingup State Forest. Dineo was so taken by what he was seeing. He insisted that Sam stopped and parked up whilst he took the opportunity too walk around amongst the trees. Sam had never seen his friend happier. Dineo was loving the silence and grandeur of the tall trees. He appeared to be totally at peace with himself. Sam watched the old man and had no intention of dragging him away. There was something about this place that Dineo connected with.

One hour later, they were pulling into the town of Narrogin. It was amazing how much it reminded them both of South Africa. So many similarities.

'Do you think Jaap may be around town Sam?'

'He could be, but I doubt it. Remember Lana said in her letters that he was having less to do with the running of the farm and that he was travelling a lot. I doubt he would want to stay here. Hopefully Karen can confirm that.'

'How are we going to approach this with Karen?' asked Dineo.

'The bottom line here is that we are looking for a man called Jaap and that we believe he owns a farm in this area. We ask her if she knows him. Then we have to play it by ear from there. It all depends on how she reacts.'

They had both read the letters and knew the history between Lana and Karen, she had conveyed lots of that to Anneline over the years. The Facebook revelations pointed to Karen as being central to Lana moving on and coupling up with Marcus. But there was a but, and it was a big one. Jaap was an evil piece of work. Sam had a strong feeling that Karen may shy away from getting involved.

Sam briefed Dineo before they left the car and headed toward the Tea Rooms. 'If she asks, then we tell her our visit is to do with the farm in South Africa. We can make it appear that we need to contact Jaap in regard to the will. If she rumbles us we will come clean. At this stage all we need to know is, if she knows where he is.'

They had agreed that Dineo would speak first. As they approached they could see Karen. The place was fairly quiet and she was standing by the till.

Karen looked up and smiled as they approached her, 'G'day fellas, table for two?'

'Yes please, can we take the one in the corner over there?'

'Sure. I'll be over in a tick to take to your order.'

As they settled at the table, Karen came over with her pad and pen in hand.

'What can I get you?'

'Pot of tea for two.' Sam replied.

Dineo followed up straight away, 'Can you help us out please, we are looking for a gentleman that we believe has a farm in this area. His name is Jaap Van NieKirk.'

Karen lowered her head to look over the top of her reading glasses, 'Oh yes, I know that bloke. But you won't find him around here anymore. He buggered off after he sold the farm a few years ago. What are you chasing him for anyway?'

Sam answered, 'His parents are recently deceased and we are trying to trace him in regard to their estate. Would you happen to know where he is now?'

'Not a bloody clue mate.'

'What about his family, we know he has a wife and son?'

'Had!' Karen corrected Sam. 'Look, let me get your teas and we can carry on with this conversation.'

Karen returned with a pot and three cups and took a seat at their table.

'His family moved away from this area too,' she informed them.

'Do you know where they went? Perhaps they can help us?'

'Leave me your card and I will try to get in touch with them for you. It'll be up to them if they want to contact you.'

Sam reacted quickest, feeling in his shirt pocket he replied, 'Oh, looks like I left my cards at the hotel. Let me give you my mobile number.'

Karen gave him her pad and he scribbled his Aussie 'pay as you go' mobile number down.

'Sorry, I am Sam, and this is Dineo.'

'Nice name, she said as she looked at Dineo. I'm Karen.'

Karen stood up to leave them and Sam said, 'Karen, please sit back down. There is something else we need to say to you.'

She sat down, 'Go on.'

'I don't know how well you knew Jaap, but I can guarantee you he isn't the person you think he is.'

Karen smiled, 'I knew him well enough to know that his wife was better off without him. But before we go any further with this, I think you better tell me who you guys really are.'

Sam decided to enlighten her, 'Fair enough. We are not looking for him in connection with his parent's estate. We are tracking him down in regard to some serious crimes he committed years ago in South Africa.'

'So you are cops?'

'No, we aren't. Karen, can we trust you?'

'If what you tell me is dinkum. Yes, you should be able to.'

'Jaap, with others, was responsible for the massacre of 32 innocent people. Dineo was there on the day that Jaap committed this crime. Fortunately, Dineo managed to escape with his life.'

Karen was clearly stunned, 'Struth mate, I knew he was a bastard, but that's knocked me for six. Oh my god, Lana. Does she know about this?'

'We don't know for sure. In all honesty, I would doubt it though.'

'Why do you say that?'

'No proof, just gut feel.' Sam paused then added, 'The massacre wasn't the only incident we know about. Dineo worked on Jaaps' father's farm and he believes Jaap murdered one of the other farm workers.'

'Good lord Dineo, that's terrible.'

Dineo spoke, 'We went back to South Africa a few weeks ago to find and confront him. That's when we found out about his parents. We found letters from Lana.'

'So you buggers already knew about her when you came in here?'

Sam answered, 'We are sorry Karen. We didn't know if we could trust you. For all we know, Jaap could still be here in town. We had to take that approach.'

'What else do you know then?'

'We know that Lana is living in Mandurah and we know of Andre. Oh yes, and we know about Marcus.'

'How the bloody hell do you know about Marcus?' Karen was astonished.

Sam smirked and said, 'You really need tighter security on your Facebook account Karen.'

They all laughed. Karen stood and offered to make more tea. The other customers had left, so now they were the only ones in the tea rooms. She passed by the front door and turned the sign to show 'closed'.

Karen looked worried as she returned to the table, 'What if Lana does know about these things? How would we know?'

'Maybe you would be able to help us find that out,' said Sam.

'Me? How?'

'Facebook to blame again Karen,' smiled Sam. 'It's clear that you guys have a special bond. You are probably the best person to ask her.'

Sam explained to Karen that they knew of Andre but not much about him.

'He's quite a private person,' said Karen.

'Is he likely to know where his father is?'

'I doubt that, he has no time for him. He excluded his father from his life years ago.'

'The last address we have for him is in Subiaco, is he still there?'

'Yeh, he still lives there. He shares a house with a couple of his mates from Narrogin. Glen and Guy, they're top blokes. I have known them since they were ankle-biters.'

Sam looked at Dineo and then Karen, 'May be worth calling in on him for a chat. But I think the best approach is the conversation with Lana first. Would you be okay with that Karen?'

'Sure, how do you want to do this?'

Sam continued, 'Sooner rather than later. I think Dineo and I should be there when you ask her. I would say no Marcus or Andre though. We have to go softly softly with this.'

'What do you want me to ask her, I mean what should I actually say?'

'Just ask her if she recalls an incident that occurred in the early eighties at the bus station in Rustenburg, where several people were killed.'

'And if she says no?'

'Then I will step in. If she says yes, then ask her what she recalls about it. Her initial reaction will tell us a lot. I just want you to crack the ice Karen. I really don't think she will lie to you. Dineo and I will take over from that point.'

'How do you want me to set up the meeting, who will I say you are?'

'We'll use the same story as we did here, tell her it's to do with the deceased estate.'

Karen suggested that she should call Lana now. Sam agreed and Karen made the call.

'Lana, it's Karen, how's it going love?'

'Karen, good thanks. What's happening?'

'I have been contacted by a couple of gentlemen, something to do with Henny and Anneline and their will.'

'Strange, why you Karen?'

'They traced Jaap to the farm here in Narrogin somehow and thought the Tea Rooms were a good place to start asking a few questions. They would like to meet with you if they could.'

'Okay, where and when?'

'How about I bring them to you? They have requested that they only want to talk to you in the first instance. Confidentiality apparently. It is okay if we come late afternoon today?'

'Fine. I'm on my own today as it happens.'

'Thanks love, they seem keen to progress with things.'

'Sure. Looking forward to seeing you.'

'Me too sweetie,' Karen replied as she completed the call.

'Terrific Karen, thanks,' said Sam.

Chapter Nineteen

⚜

Sam and Dineo agreed with Karen to travel separately and meet in Mandurah before going to Lana's house. As they met at the rear of the property Sam asked Karen, 'Are you good to go as planned?'

'No worries Sam.'

Lana opened the door and hugged her friend, then she looked at Sam and Dineo.

She seemed to take a longer look at Dineo, not as if she recognised him, more like she knew where he was from.

'Excuse me gentlemen, 'I am Lana, and you are?'

They introduced themselves with a handshake and followed the ladies into the house at Lana's request.

'Are you coffee drinkers gents, I have just brewed a fresh pot?'

Sam responded, 'We are and it smells great, thank you.'

They settled on the sofas, the same ones where Andre had broken the sad news weeks before.

Sam broke the silence, 'First of all, can we offer you our condolences on your sad loss.'

Lana nodded appreciatively. Sam looked at Karen as a cue. Sam watched Lana carefully to monitor her response.

'Lana, there is something we need to ask you. Do you recall an incident that occurred in the early eighties at the bus station in Rustenburg, where several people were killed?'

Lana was clearly puzzled at the question from her friend but showed no sign of nerves. The question did not trigger a response that could be associated with guilt or shame.

Lana slowly looked at all of them in turn and responded, 'If you mean the attack where 32 people lost their lives, yes I remember that.'

Once again Sam looked at Karen.

Karen was very tempted to reach out and touch her friends' hand but resisted, 'Can you recall what actually happened?'

'Everything I learned came from what others had told me,' Lana started, then putting her hand to her mouth said, 'Oh my god, you don't think that is linked to what happened to Anneline and Henny?'

Sam interjected, 'We don't think so Lana. But we would like to know what you know about the attack at the bus station.'

This time Karen did reach out and hold Lana's hand, as she recognised her friend's breathing had changed. Lana composed herself and continued, 'We were having a Braai at Rustenburg Kloof. I must have been only 17 at the time and had just started dating Jaap. We were there with all of his friends and their wives or girlfriends. I remember it was a lovely evening. The first indication we had that something had happened was when two policemen arrived at The Kloof. They circulated through the groups of people saying that there had been some civil unrest in the town and it was now under control, but we must all take extreme care when travelling home.'

Sam asked, 'And Jaap and the other men were with you all of the time?'

'Yes,' Lana hesitated, then added, 'Well, we ladies got to the Kloof before them. The boys went into town to pick up the drinks.'

Sam asked, 'Could you ever believe it possible that Jaap may have been involved in that attack?'

Her response showed an edge of innocence that convinced Sam that she did not know that Jaap was capable of such things.

'My marriage to Jaap was a roller coaster, highs and lows that I am sure many people never experience. But he was never violent to me and I really don't believe he would have it in him to do anything like that.'

Sam knew it was time to come clean and tell Lana why they were actually there. Had Karen not been there he would never have asked Dineo to say what he was about to say.

'Lana, we are not here to discuss the family estate. Dineo, could you please tell Lana who you are and why we need her help?'

'I have known Jaap since he was 17 years old when I worked on his father's farm. I left the farm, but I did not forget him. On the day of the attack I was driving a bus, and I looked him in the eyes as he and the others massacred our passengers.'

Lana said nothing, she looked stunned as she listened to Dineo. Her bottom lip started to quiver and her eyes were filling up with tears. Karen moved around to sit with her and placed her arm around her.

'How, how do I not know this? How could Jaap have kept this from me? Am I that gullible?'

'Not gullible Lana. Trusting perhaps? There is possibly lots of things you don't know about him,' said Sam

Lana stood, and with tears rolling down her cheeks, came over to Dineo and hugged him. 'I am so, so sorry Dineo.'

Dineo responded, 'You have nothing to apologise for.'

She held him close for a few seconds then leaned back to look into his eyes. 'How can I help you now?'

'I need to look into his eyes once again. He has to be accountable for what he has done.'

'Do you know where he is Lana?' asked Sam.

'I have no idea, I am sorry.'

'What about Andre, is he likely to know?'

'He has nothing to do with his father anymore. But it may be worth asking him,' said Lana.

Once again, Sam requested if a meeting could be arranged on the same terms. Andre did not have to know the real reason they were looking for him. Lana called Andre and asked him if the two men could come and visit him.

'Sure mum. We are just hanging out at home tonight anyway. Tell them I will be expecting them.'

Sam stood and indicated for Dineo to follow him, 'Thanks Lana, will you be okay?'

'Karen will stay with me this evening. Should we tell Marcus?'

'I think you can answer that one better than me Lana.'

Lana acknowledged Sam's respect for her relationship with a smile.

'I will call you when I finish talking with Andre, we can take things from there.'

'Good luck gentlemen,' Lana said as she saw them to the door.

Dineo turned to Lana and Karen and said, 'Thank you both.'

—◆—

Andre jumped up off the sofa as he saw the car pull onto the driveway. He opened the front door, 'Come in fellas, not sure if I can be of much help, but fire away with your questions.'

Glen and Guy were lounging back on another sofa and were engaged in a play station game on their big screen television.

'Turn the volume down a bit guys,' said Andre.

'Yeh, no worries mate,' replied Guy.

Andre addressed his visitors once again. 'Sorry fellas, how can I help you?'

'We would like to contact your father in connection with your Grandparents estate. And please accept our condolences for your loss Andre.'

Glen paused the game and asked Guy to go get them another couple of stubbies from the fridge. Andre nodded his appreciation in regard to his loss and replied, 'I have no idea where that bastard is, what's more I don't want to know.'

Guy returned with five stubbies and offered them around to everyone. He sat down and went to restart the game, but Glen blocked him and nodded toward the conversation that was going on.

Sam thanked Guy and looked back at Andre, 'When was the last time you had contact with him?'

'Jeez, easy eight or nine years. Since I left the farm really.'

'And you haven't seen him since then?'

'No, not at all.'

'Lying bastard,' chirped Guy.

Andre looked over at Guy with a surprised expression.

Guy prompted him, 'We seen the old bastard on TV, the Grand Final, remember?'

Andre burst out laughing, 'Oh yeh, I forgot about that.'

Sam didn't want to miss an opportunity, 'The Grand Final, he wasn't playing was he?'

His comment brought a round of laughter from around the room.

Andre looked on as Guy responded first, 'Not on the field mate.'

Sam raised his eyes to Guy to encourage him to continue.

'He was up to no good with the Freo mafia mate. We picked him out in the crowd, they were in one of those expensive hospitality boxes.'

'Who is the Freo mafia?' asked Sam.

Glen cut in and pointed at the TV screen and said to Guy, 'Are we gonna play this fucking game or what mate?'

Andre stood and led Sam and Dineo to the rear patio as his two friends restarted their game.

'Sorry fellas, I really don't think I can help you any further.'

Sam signalled to Dineo to finish off their beers and replied to Andre, 'Not to worry, we will try some other avenues of investigation.'

Andre led them round to the front driveway and leaned into the driver's side of the car, 'If you do find him, I would appreciate if you did not let him know where I am.'

'Don't worry Andre, we wouldn't do that,' Sam reassured him.

—∿∿—

Sam pulled away and stopped the car 20 metres up the road, all the time watching for Andre to enter the house. He scribbled the address of a hotel on a piece of paper, together with his mobile number, but included one incorrect digit in the phone number. He told Dineo to wait for him. He walked back to the house and waited until he could see only Guy and Glen in the main living area. He rang the doorbell once again and Glen answered this time.

He handed the piece of paper to Glen, 'Hey, sorry to disturb you, but I meant to give this to Andre. We will be staying at this address for a couple of days, if you could let him know please. If he remembers anything, please ask him to get in touch.'

'I sure will mate,' replied the smiling Glen.

Sam walked back to the car, climbed in and said to Dineo, 'If we can't find Jaap, then perhaps he should find us?'

Dineo gave him one of his 'I am sure you know what you are talking about looks.'

'Mr. V. Just wanted to let you know, there's a couple of blokes been asking about after you. A white Pommie and a black South African.'

'Really, when and where?'

'They came to the house to speak with Andre, they left about twenty minutes ago.'

'What did they want?'

'They were looking for you, something to do with your parents' estate in South Africa. Don't worry, they left with nothing. I managed to find out where they are staying though.'

'Good job Glen, pass it on to Goran. Tell him to keep me in the loop. I want to know who these folks are and what they want.'

'Sure Mr. V.'

Sam stopped the car a couple of streets away from Andre's place. He phoned The Esplanade Hotel in Fremantle and confirmed his reservation and he requested a twin room, front facing on the first floor. Then he called Lana.

'Hi Lana, it's Sam, are you okay to talk now?'

'Hi Sam, yes I am, how did it go?'

'No joy with Andre. There was something you may be able to help me with though.'

'Fire away,' replied Lana.

'Maybe a bit of a strange one, but who are the Freo Mafia?'

'My goodness, I wouldn't have a clue.'

'Can you ask Karen?' Sam paused then added, 'Or maybe Marcus will know. Is he home with you now?'

'Yes, he is.'

'Better still, can we come and visit with you all in the morning? It would be good to meet Marcus in person so he can hear things directly from us. Will that be okay?'

'Come and have breakfast with us, say 9 am?'

'Perfect. Hold off on the Mafia thing until we meet. Thank you. See you then.'

They arrived at the Esplanade hotel and checked in.

'Oh sir, you had a visitor a few minutes ago.'

Sam asked the young male receptionist, 'Did he leave a name?'

The young man looked at the computer screen in front of him, 'No sir, no forwarding number either. He said he would call back later though.'

'Thank you.' Sam took a few steps away from the reception then turned back and looked up at the black CCTV sphere positioned over in the corner behind the desk.

He quietly asked the young man, 'It would be so helpful if I could see who it was. Is that camera on?'

'Yes, but it wouldn't be right for me to show you any images.'

Sam tried his hand, 'Look, I shouldn't tell you this, but this gentleman with me is in protective custody. It's really important that I see who that was.'

The receptionist looked at Dineo then looked around the foyer of the hotel to ensure none of his managers were watching. Then he turned his attention to the computer. After a few seconds he swung the monitor around so Sam could view the image on the screen. Sam took a shot of the image with the camera on his phone.

'Thank you so much,' he said as he slid the young man $20.

Sam took one of the hotel business cards from the desk and wrote his mobile number on the back. He handed it back to the receptionist and said, 'If this guy comes back, do not tell him what room we are in, or even if we are in the hotel. Just call me and let me know that he is here, but be discrete. Can you put a note on your system to say that please?'

'Yes sir, that's not a problem.'

The young man felt rather pleased with himself as he watched his new guests walk towards the lifts.

—<small>᠊ᢔᢘᢕᢘᢕ</small>—

On the journey down to Mandurah, Sam explained to Dineo why the dynamic had changed and how they were playing by a different set of rules.

'We came here looking for a man that had committed crimes in the past and our goal was to face him as reasonable human beings and challenge him. This was about your conscience and ridding yourself of any guilt associated with what you had witnessed.' It's gone beyond that now.'

Dineo needed further explanation, 'How do you know that?'

'They trained me to be a killer Dineo. They trained me to think fast and react faster. Never switching off, they finely tuned my intuition. It's impossible to unlearn that. I witnessed things at Andre's place that has convinced me that we need to be concerned.'

Dineo remembered Sam's account of his time in the Special Forces.

Sam continued, 'Andre knew nothing and didn't care. Guy knew something and was about to tell, and Glen was controlling the conversation in the room.'

Dineo thought back to the meeting at Andre's place, 'I see where you are coming from now.'

'I would stake my life on it that Jaap has progressed from the killer in the past to the villain of today. Glen was protecting him, I set a trap and he fell for it.'

'Our visitor last night?'

'Exactly. We have to move fast Dineo, it's not just us that are at risk. Anyone that can draw attention to Jaap and whatever he is involved in is at risk. You know as well as I do, he will do anything to protect himself. It's all about him.'

They arrived at Lana's place and pulled onto the driveway.

'Four car driveway and a garage that can hold another two, that's ultra luxury in the UK Dineo.'

—

Goran carried on past them. It was always going to be easy for him, a black man and a white man in a red hire car that was parked overnight in the Esplanade Hotel car park. It was made even easier for him when Glen forwarded the photo of them standing on the patio at the house in Subiaco. It was also a bit of a given that they would be going to Lana's place.

Jaap had picked up on Glen's vulnerability when he was a 10-year-old and at school with Andre. Glen had lost his father in a tragic road accident when he was a six-year-old and there was a distinct lack of male role models in his life. Narrogin was a small country town, so Glen's mother had to be extra discrete in her liaisons with Jaap. She loved the attention that he was giving to her son and was eternally grateful for the kind handouts that Jaap provided each month. It was hard raising a child with the small amount of income she was bringing in. She did not love Jaap, but certainly appreciated him and that bought her loyalty and silence.

Lana greeted them on the driveway and ushered them into her home. Marcus was standing in the hallway as they entered.

'Gentlemen, this is my lovely Marcus.'

Marcus shook hands in turn with them, 'I hope you blokes are hungry, we are having a barbie breakfast and it's fully loaded.'

'We will try not to let you down Marcus,' said Sam.

'Good on ya, come through,' Marcus led them through the side door and onto the paved outside sitting area.

Karen was already there, she looked up as they stepped towards the table she was seated at, 'G'day fellas. How's it going?'

Dineo responded, 'We are good thank you.'

Karen stood and greeted them with a peck on their cheeks.

Jaap had just sat down to have lunch with Debbie. They were at a prestigious harbour front restaurant at Milsons Point. Jaap's phone buzzed on the table, he looked down and saw it was Goran. He picked up the phone as he stood to take the call away from the table. He looked at Debbie and she rolled her eyes at him.

He stared back at her and growled, 'Oh really?'

He answered as he walked to look out at the splendid views of Sydney harbour, 'Goran, howzit?'

'Hey Jaap, all good here. Your mystery men are visiting your ex in Mandurah.'

'Did you get a photo?'

'Sending it now, Glen took it yesterday.'

'Then why the fuck did you not send it yesterday?' Jaap raged back at him.

Goran very much worked for Jaap now, despite their beginnings, things had turned around dramatically once Jaap had access to the Melbourne Mafia heads.

'Sorry boss.'

'Pick your game up man,' Jaap warned him as he opened the attached image. 'I don't recognise these men. The black one is definitely from the Northern Transvaal though. He has that look about him. Are you any wiser about why they want to see me?'

'Nothing more than you already know from Glen, Jaap.'

'Okay, keep a close eye on them and let me know if I need to get involved. Right?'

'Message understood boss.'

Jaap returned to the table to a sheepish looking Debbie, 'You will do well to remember how I picked you up out of your shit life. There's always a quick return to it, anytime you choose.'

—⁓—

Lana did her best to make Dineo feel welcome in her home. They chatted continuously through breakfast, whilst Karen listened on, only losing her when Lana switched to the fair amount of Tswana that she still remembered. Karen could see that Dineo had warmed to Lana. His smile was genuine.

Sam had been sounding out Marcus, although he was not wary of him, he needed to get a solid footing to begin the more serious discussion that was on its way.

A cool breeze was channelling down the side of the house and Lana suggested that they retire inside where it would be more comfortable. 'How about I make us a fresh pot of coffee and we sit down together for a talk?'

Everyone showed their approval and began taking seats around the huge dining table.

It was Marcus that opened the conversation, 'This is a terrible business about Jaap.'

'How much do you know?' Sam asked him.

Lana interjected, 'He knows everything Sam.'

Sam and Dineo had agreed not to mention Glen at this time. It was clear from a previous conversation with Karen that she had a liking for him. No need to burst that bubble just yet.

Sam was keen to push things along, 'Okay, this may sound like a strange question, but who runs organised crime out of Fremantle?'

Both Karen and Marcus looked keen to answer but Marcus spoke first, 'Growing up as a Perth boy, it was always the ethnic groups, Italians, and people from the former Yugoslavian countries mainly. It's a bit more inclusive now though. But if you're looking for the more professional outfits, then stick with the Croats and the Italians on a smaller scale, they are both governed from the Eastern States.'

'Thanks Marcus, that's very helpful, Karen, were you going to say something?'

'Just what Marcus said really. It is becoming more of a problem.'

'Why do you ask anyway Sam, do you think Jaap may be involved?'

'There's nothing solid to go on, but to be honest with you, yes, I do think he may be involved on some level.'

Sam did not want to reveal to Lana that he and Dineo had read all of her letters to Anneline, so he tactfully asked, 'Lana, can you give me a brief history of Jaap's business interests since you arrived from South Africa?'

'Sure,' she replied.

Before she could start in earnest, Marcus stood and asked, 'Gents, are you partial to a drop of red?'

Karen jumped in, 'I don't know about the blokes, but I am.'

Sam laughed and replied, 'That would be lovely Marcus, thanks.'

Dineo declined the offer.

Lana continued as Marcus poured the drinks, 'It was nothing but the farm at first. Then he moved on to second hand farming equipment sales. After that, he started travelling a lot and said he was looking at partnerships with people in the Eastern States, something to do with distribution of chemicals used in the farming industry. To be honest, I started paying less attention to what he was doing as that was the time Karen and I started up our business together.'

'Strangely enough, I knew about him before I even met Lana and Karen,' said Marcus.

Sam asked. 'Yes? How was that?'

'I was a regional sales manager for new farming machinery in Western Australia. Occasionally, some of my clients would talk about him and how they had offloaded some of their older machinery to his company.'

'What was the company name Marcus, can you remember?'

'Yes, it was McGuire Agricultural Holdings.'

'Okay, let's check that out,' Sam said as he walked over to get his trusty laptop. They all moved round to watch Sam search for registered business names in Australia. He located McGuire Agricultural Holdings within a few seconds and clicked on the link to view the details of the company directors. Karen responded first as she shouted out, 'Sandra bloody McGuire, oh my forefathers.'

Everyone turned to her for an explanation.

'She's only the most notorious madam in Kalgoorlie.'

'And Jaap was in business with her?' asked Lana.

'Still could be,' Sam added.

Sam performed another search to find out what other businesses Sandra was involved in at Director level. It was a short list and it was Lana that noticed it first.

'She owns the farm.'

Sam was slightly confused, 'Excuse me?'

'Click on that name there Sam.'

Sam clicked on a link to 'Vaalrivier,' and it opened another page.

It was now evident that Jaap had sold the farm to a company where Sandra was a Director. They all sat back in silence for a short while until Sam asked, 'What is the farm now?'

'What do you mean Sam?'

'Sorry Lana, I mean is it still a farm?'

Karen responded, 'No Sam, it's derelict, has been for years. Such a waste.'

Sam closed his laptop and declared, 'I think we need to pay a visit to the farm.'

Sam noticed that Dineo had nodded off to sleep.

Karen kindly offered Sam and Dineo an overnight stay at her place in Narrogin. Dineo could stay with her while Sam went to take a late night look around the farm. Sam was delighted, he was growing concerned about Dineo's general fitness level and certainly did not want to put him in harms way if he could avoid it.

Once again, Karen travelled in her own car. She gave her address to Sam to enter into his GPS, they would meet up at her place.

Chapter Twenty One

Goran had placed a vehicle tracking device on Sam's car. As soon as the car started moving, he would be notified through the app on his phone. At 7pm he received the notification that the car was heading out of Mandurah. He left the remains of the coffee he had been enjoying at the cafe on the Freo Cappuccino strip and got into his car. He placed his phone in the holder and tracked the journey that the red hire car was making. After watching for twenty minutes he knew where the car was headed. He phoned Glen.

'Hey Glen, where are you mate?'

'At home.'

'Meet me in Narrogin, get there as soon as you can. Park outside the Post Office.'

Two hours later and all parties had arrived in Narrogin.

Glen sat in Goran's car and monitored the tracking app.

'They are outside of Karen's place,' said Glen.

Sam and Karen discussed the location of the farm while Dineo settled in front of the TV and relaxed.

Karen touched Sam on his forearm, 'Be careful Sam.'
'Will do, keep an eye on the old fella please.'

—⁓—

The tracker kicked in again, the hire car was moving. Goran slowly edged his car forward and followed Sam.

'He's heading out toward the farm,' said Glen.

Goran didn't reply, he just looked nervously at Glen.

'There's only one of them in the car,' noted Glen.

Goran stopped his car, 'Go back Glen. Pick up your car and keep an eye on Karen's place. The other one must be there.'

It only took Glen a few minutes to run back and collect his car. He drove around to Karen's place and parked up with the lights off. He had a good view into her living room.

—⁓—

Sam drove past the main entrance to the farm. He had seen that the main entrance gate was chained up with a 'No Entry Private Property' sign on it. Goran had stopped following him, the lights would be a giveaway and he had the tracker anyway. Sam pulled off the road 40 meters after the main entrance gate and parked up. He walked to the perimeter fence of the farm and took out his night vision binoculars.

There was no sign of life. He needed to get a view of the farm buildings, so he climbed over the fence and walked through the rows of trees that fronted the farm. As soon as Goran detected that Sam's car had come to a stop, he killed his engine. He was close enough to catch up on foot. He texted Glen, *'He's snooping around the farm. inform Jaap.'*

Sam reached a good vantage point, lay flat, and lifted his night visions to his eyes once more. There was nothing to be seen or heard, apart from the constant sound of the insects of the night. Goran found Sam's car and stopped and listened carefully for any sound of movement and heard nothing. But Sam's trained ear picked up the sound of someone trying to be quiet. He turned and looked back to where he had detected the noise. He zoomed in on the face with his night visions, it was the same one he had seen on the security image at the hotel.

Goran was standing at the perimeter fence with Sam's car behind him when he read the text as it came in from Jaap, *'Too close to home. stop them.'*

Sam avoided laughing out loud as Goran's phone lit up his face.

Glen received the text from Jaap at the same time. He knew what his task was and Karen was in the way.

Sam had already prioritised his course of action. Immobilise the immediate threat and ensure the safety of Dineo. He picked up a large stone and threw it as hard as he could at the car window, as soon as he heard the crack against the glass, he activated the car alarm on the remote. Goran ducked for cover and drew his weapon, training it on the trees straight ahead of him. Sam moved as fast as he could to Goran's right. Goran was now panicking, thinking he had been shot at. The car alarm was screaming behind him providing cover for any noise that Sam was making as he circled round, he crossed the perimeter fence and positioned himself behind Goran. Sam grabbed a handful of gravel, crept up behind the car, turned on the torch on his mobile phone and threw it over the fence to right of Goran. As Goran reacted, Sam closed in on him and kicked him in the back of his knee. Goran fell to the floor and turned to face Sam. As he turned, Sam threw the gravel into his eyes. Sam kicked the gun out of Goran's hand and punched him in the throat as hard as he could.

As Goran lay on the ground rubbing his eyes and clutching his throat, Sam recovered the weapon, turned off the car alarm and said, 'That noise is very distracting isn't it pal?'

Sam picked up Goran's phone, 'Okay asshole, what's the code?'

Goran returned a muffled, 'Fuck you'.

Sam placed the end of the gun barrel on Goran's eyeball and asked him, 'Is this a real gun Mister?'

'1 9 9 0,' came the immediate reply from Goran.

Sam tapped in the code and it worked. He put the phone in his pocket.

'Where's your vehicle?'

'Parked up by the main gate.'

'Take your belt off.'

Goran removed his waist belt and dropped it on the ground.

'Turn over, face in the dirt.'

As Goran rolled over, Sam took the belt and wrapped it around his ankles in a figure eight, pulled it as tight as he could and secured it.

'Sorry about this pal.'

'About what?' Asked Goran.

Sam dislocated the index fingers on both of Goran's hands.

'That.'

Sam ejected the boot of the car and dragged Goran over. He lifted him in and slammed it shut. It was hard to hear his screaming now. He would figure out what to do with Goran later, but for now, he had to get back to Karen and Dineo. He recovered his own phone, then set off for Karen's place. As he drove off, Goran's phone buzzed in Sam's pocket, he stopped and looked at it. The app was telling him that his car was moving. Sam started to laugh uncontrollably, probably down to the amount of adrenalin that was coursing through his veins. He stopped and got out of the car and walked to the passenger side rear wheel arch and removed the sender. As he walked past the car boot he banged on it and shouted, 'Did your mafia pals send you to the Boy Scouts for training?'

He passed by the red Lamborghini at the main gate of the farm, it was okay there for now, he thought.

As Sam arrived at Karen's home, he saw that her front door was open. He felt the pang of caution kick in and he approached slowly and quietly. He saw her feet first. She was lying face down in her hallway and she had a wound to the side of her head. He shouted for Dineo and there was no response. Turning back to Karen, he called her name. She responded straight away, he rolled her over into the recovery position and asked her what happened.

'There was a knock on the door and I went to answer. That's all I remember.'

'Where is Dineo, Karen?'

'He's watching TV.'

Sam walked into the living room and saw the upturned coffee table and Dineo's phone on the floor. He checked out the rest of the house and it was clear. Dineo had been taken.

CHAPTER TWENTY TWO

Sam helped Karen onto the sofa and inspected her head wound. There was more bruising than blood, but she would need to go to hospital and have it checked out. He had to establish his next move. Karen was fine for the moment.

Goran's phone buzzed. Karen looked on as Sam read the incoming text. *'Where are you? I have the old man with me.'*

'Whose phone is that?' Karen was confused.

'It belongs to a bloke that is in the boot of my car.'

'Okay, that makes sense,' Karen sniggered.

'That's a bit of a long story Karen, sorry. Let me see who is texting him.'

Sam followed the stream of texts back and informed Karen.

'You were attacked by Glen. It's Glen that has Dineo.'

'What?'

'He is working for Jaap. I had my suspicions but needed some proof, and it's here. Jaap is pulling the strings from wherever he is.'

Karen found it hard to believe that the nice child she had witnessed growing up could have attacked her.

'Who's the man in your boot Sam?'

'He is Freo Mafia,' Sam showed an image of Goran to Karen, 'that's him.'

'I have seen this bloke, he's been to Narrogin many times.'

All the time Sam was talking to Karen, he was thinking about what he should text back. He had to keep the conversation going with Glen and he needed to respond as if he was Goran. Sam logged on to his laptop and connected Goran's phone and started the process of backing up everything from the phone. Then he replied to the text, being careful to adopt the same conversational style of previous messages between Goran and Glen.

'Taking care of our other friend. where are you?'

Glen replied, *'At the holding point.'*

Sam looked at Karen, 'Wow, that's helpful. Not!'

'Why don't you ask the guy in the boot?'

'We need to keep him well and truly out of the loop Karen. The less he knows, the better.'

Karen was in awe of how Sam was managing things.

Sam said, 'This will be a bit of a gamble, but here goes.'

He texted. *'I will meet you there. stay put.'*

The reply came back, *'Hurry then. I think this old bloke may kark it. He put up a bit of fight when I took him.'*

Karen and Sam exchanged worried glances at each other. A noise was coming from the boot of Sam's car.

Karen looked towards the noise and said, 'You have to go ask him Sam, we have to get to Dineo quickly.'

'Do you have any spirits in the house?'

'Plenty, what do you fancy?'

'It's not for me, I think a cheap whiskey will do the trick.'

Karen grabbed a bottle and joined Sam out at his car. Sam popped the boot, uncapped the whiskey and poured the whole bottle down Goran's throat. Then slammed the boot shut.

Karen looked on with amazement, 'What's going on mate?'

'Give him a few minutes.'

Sam walked back in the house and checked the laptop. It had finished transferring all the files from the phone. He had a quick look through the folders, everything was there, pictures, messages, contacts, emails and all the data anyone would need to unpick Goran's villainous dealings. He shut the laptop down and handed it to Karen, 'Keep this somewhere safe, if anything happens to me it's going to come in useful. The password is DINEO.'

'Now. Let's check on our pal in the boot.'

Sam popped the boot and reached into Goran's pocket for his car keys. Goran was looking quite happy considering his situation.

Sam tried some trickery. 'Hey pal, tell me again where the holding point is.'

'Fuck you,' came the reply from the intoxicated laughing Goran.

'I may have over cooked that one,' Sam said as he slammed the boot closed. 'Let's get this car into your garage Karen.'

Once they had secured the car in the garage Sam said, 'We need to get you to the hospital. Is there anyone you can call to take you there?'

'Sergeant Thompson.'

'No cops Karen. We can't afford to have them plodding in yet.'

'Where is the hospital?'

'About 3 Kilometres past the farm entrance.'

'Great, drop me at the farm entrance and you carry on to the hospital. Are you up to it?'

'Yes, I feel fine.'

'You may feel okay now but promise me you will go to the hospital.'

'Promise. What are you going to do?'

'Trick Glen into meeting me hopefully.'

———

As Karen pulled up at the farm entrance, Sam texted Glen. *'Problem. need your help. meet me at the farm entrance. urgent.'*

Glen replied, *'WTF?'*

'Just get here.'

'What about the old boy?'

'Leave him there. Hurry.'

'I think this may work, now get yourself off to the hospital,' Sam said to Karen.

Sam jumped out and told Karen he would call her as soon as he could. He watched Karen drive off, she was doing fine, well in control of the car. He tried the remote on Goran's car, it was working fine. While he waited, he went through the photos on Goran's phone. He would enjoy taking a more detailed look later.

Ten minutes, and still no Glen. He thought about sending another text and held off just as he spotted the headlights appearing to his left.

Sam was lying behind a bush on the opposite side of the road to Goran's car. Sam took out Goran's gun and readied it for use.

Glen pulled up behind Goran's car. Sam watched him carefully as he opened the door and stepped out into the road. Just as he did, Sam started the engine of the Lamborghini with the remote. As Glen stepped forward to look inside the car Sam shot him in his right thigh. His leg buckled under him and he fell to the floor. Sam ran over to him and dragged him off the road and onto the red dust verge on the other side of the car.

By now Glen was screaming, 'You bastard, you shot me.'

'That's nothing compared to what Karen is going to do you mate. Hope you are not planning on having kids pal,' Sam said as he laughed at him.

'Get me to the hospital.'

'Not happening pal. It's just a flesh wound, you'll survive. But I'll tell you this, if anything happens to my friend, I am going to kill you slowly, do you understand?'

'Yes,' came his pathetic reply.

'I need your phone and the code and don't make me ask for it twice.'

Glen surrendered his phone and the code without any resistance.

'Now, you have a choice, I can cram you into the tiny boot or you can travel in the passenger seat, what's it gonna be?'

'In the car please.'

Sam checked the messages on Glen's phone. It revealed the same as Goran's phone. Recent messaging was confined to Jaap, Glen and Goran. No one else appeared to be involved.

'Okay, get me to the holding point. No tricks.'

Sam had searched Glen before he got into the car, he was not carrying a weapon.

'What's going to happen to me?' he sheepishly asked Sam.

'Kidnap, serious assault, and that's without looking at the evidence on your phone. You will probably miss the best years of your life pal.'

Glen started to weep, 'I never meant to get in this deep.'

'Sure', said Sam, 'Heard it all before mate.'

Sam saw an opportunity, 'How deep are you in Glen?'

'If I tell you will it help?'

'Dunno, but you're fucked anyway pal.' Sam paused then said, 'Show me you can do the right thing Glen and I'll do what I can for you.'

They had only been driving for five minutes when Glen declared, 'Turn left, we are here.'

Sam guessed they were somewhere at the back of the farm. They pulled up alongside a farm shed. Sam helped Glen hobble round to a side door where they made their entrance.

Once inside, Glen pointed at an electrical fuse box, 'Remove the third fuse on the left.'

As Sam did so, a section of the floor slid away revealing a stairway.

'Your friend is in there.'

This would be the first test for Glen. Sam walked over to the stairway and made his way down. Dineo lay on the floor amongst various containers of chemicals that were neatly stacked around him. Sam listened for any indication that Glen was attempting to close the hatchway. So far, so good. He moved quickly over to Dineo. His friend was sweating profusely, and his breathing was shallow. Sam gave him a fireman's lift and climbed out of the underground storage area.

Glen looked at Sam, 'Is he going to be okay?'

'We need to get him to the hospital,' Sam looked at Glen's leg, 'And you too.'

They left the shed as they had found it and as they stepped outside Sam said. 'Oh shit, it's a Lamborghini.'

'Take him mate, come back for me.'

Sam looked Glen in the eyes, they were full of tears, 'Okay, I won't be long. In the meantime, think up a story that you are going to tell them at the hospital of how you came to be shot.'

Glen smiled, 'Will do.'

Sam took stock of the situation, three people in hospital and a drunken Croatian in the boot of his car, not a bad night's work. He spoke with the senior nurse on night duty. Karen was fine, they would be keeping her in overnight for observation and she would be discharged in the morning, all being well. Glen had a flesh wound to his thigh, the bullet had passed through without creating too much damage. He would eventually make a good recovery.

The nurse asked Sam how well he knew Dineo and what his relationship was with him.

'We are friends, we are on vacation together from the UK. Why, is there a problem?'

'Can we take a seat over here please?' she asked him.

Sam was getting worried.

'How much do you know about his condition?'

Sam didn't want to give anything away about what had gone on during the night, 'That's how I found him. I realised he had suffered some sort of trauma and I brought him straight here.'

'Sorry, I don't mean what he is dealing with in regard to what's happened this evening. I am talking about his ongoing health issue.'

'I was not aware that he has an ongoing health issue.' Sam was becoming agitated, 'Look, he has no one else, I am his closest friend. Could you please tell me what's going on?'

'He is not a well man. He has a brain tumour and it is in its final stages. Whatever has happened this evening has weakened him greatly.'

Sam was tired, it had been a long day and he was exhausted by the events of the evening. He was coming down from his adrenaline rush and now he was trying to process what the nurse was saying to him.

'What are you actually saying, is he going to make it?'

'The Consultant will see him in the morning, we will know better then.'

'Can I see him please?'

'You can visit him for a short while, we have sedated him, so he will be a little groggy. I'll take you through.'

'Thank you.'

Dineo was lying on his back and propped up slightly, he opened his eyes as they walked into his room.

The nurse stood at the door and watched Sam walk over to his bed, 'Keep it to five minutes or so please.'

'Hey pal, how's it going?' Sam said as he rubbed Dineo's forearm.

'Oh, I am well Sam,' he replied in his normal positive way.

'Did Glen hurt you Dineo?'

'No, not at all. I gave him a right hook and fell over in the process.'

The friends shared a laugh for a few moments.

'What about this other business Dineo, your tumour, why didn't you tell me?'

'Because I'm having too much fun Sam,' replied Dineo with a huge smile.

Sam felt the lump in his throat and turned away, he didn't want his friend to witness him getting emotional.

With his face turned away, Sam took a deep breath and asked him, 'Is there anything I can get you?'

'No, they are taking care of me just fine.'

Sam stood up and said, 'Get some rest. I will be back for you in the morning. Sleep well pal.'

'Night Sam, and thank you.'

Sam winked, smiled and left the room.

As he walked out to the car park, the phones belonging to Goran and Glen buzzed simultaneously in his pockets. He took them out and looked at the message from Jaap.

'WTF is going on. update me!'

He responded with Goran's phone, '*Problem resolved. no ongoing threat.*'

The reply came straight back. *'Good. talk tomorrow'*

It was close to 2am. Sam spent the night in the Lamborghini. He had reclined the seat and fell into a deep sleep that comes with exhaustion, both mental and physical. He woke at 6:30am and his first thought was for his friend. Had he brought this on by pushing Dineo too much? Dragging him around two continents at the other end of the world? He felt a great sadness inside. Had he taken the wrong that was done to Dineo and personalised it? Did he have any right to do that?

He walked into the hospital and selected a coffee from a vending machine. As he waited for it to be dispensed, he heard the ambulance sirens outside. The big perspex external doors swung open and a trolley came through carrying a young teenage girl. In less than ten minutes, he learned that she had died as a result of taking some illicit substance at a friend's party. He looked at his watch, he thought that her parents would probably still be sleeping, unaware of the day that was about to greet them. Once again, Sam sat down to think of the way forward.

CHAPTER TWENTY FOUR

Glen managed the operation at Vaalrivier. The location was perfect, an abandoned farm with its main buildings well back and out of sight from the road. The underground mining operation had been overseen by a client of Sandra's. An old mining engineer with many skeletons in his cupboard, discretion guaranteed. The underground workings were directly below the homestead but not accessed through it. There were two access or egress points. One for people, and the other for product. Both were cleverly designed and heavily concealed. Product would leave through an inclined shaft at the rear of the property and travel 200 metres upwards to the exit. The exit connected directly with a service road at the rear of the farm, which in turn led to a rarely used tar road behind the farm. This ensured any comings and goings were well away from prying eyes of the townsfolk. Product was always moved under the cover of darkness to minimise any risk of detection.

Karen had negotiated an early discharge for Glen on the condition that she would look after him. He was resting with his leg and had it elevated on a recliner seat in Karen's living room. It was 10am and Glen had just made his confession to Sam and Karen at her home.

Karen didn't know whether to cry or scream, 'Do you have any idea what you have done Glen?'

'I've been so stupid Karen, I am so sorry.'

'Stupidity does not come anywhere near it mate,' she fired back at him.

Sam stood up and said to Karen, 'We better go check in the garage.'

As they stepped away, Glen asked, 'What's going to happen to me?'

Sam replied, 'Leave that with us Glen, I gave you my word I would help if you came good. But what you have just told us has shifted this up a league or two. Sit still for now.'

Sam stopped at the entrance to Karen's garage, 'How well do you know this Sergeant Thompson, Karen?'

'Intimately, may be the best way to describe it,' she smirked.

'Oh, okay. We need to involve him as soon as possible. But I have some conditions.'

Karen used the remote to open the garage door and Sam popped the boot. The air became heavy with the smell of whiskey and urine.

'How was your evening sir?' Sam asked their guest sarcastically.

Goran was in no mood to respond and didn't.

'Give him a bottle of water and some Paracetamol Karen. He can have a lie in this morning.'

They returned to join Glen inside after securing Goran in the boot once more.

'We will be able to undo some of this mess for you Glen, but I have to be straight with you. It is inevitable there will be a price to pay. What do you want to do?'

Glen hung his head, 'Whatever I have to do. I want out.'

'Where is Jaap, Glen?' Sam asked.

'He lives in Sydney now.'

'Does he come back over here?'

'Only for something urgent.'

'Like what?'

'If someone needs to be disciplined.'

They all knew what Glen meant by that remark.

Sam informed Glen, 'He texted Goran last night to say they would talk today. That may be a little awkward for us, any ideas how we get around that, so we don't arouse his suspicions?'

'I could call him and tell him that Goran has gone on a bender.'

Sam and Karen laughed simultaneously, and Karen said, 'Well, that wouldn't be strictly untrue.'

Glen looked puzzled.

'Later,' Sam said.

Sam briefed Glen on what to say on the call to Jaap. The call went well, Jaap seemed relaxed and okay with the situation. As far as he knew, Vaalrivier was in silent running mode and the threat posed by the visitors was no longer a concern.

'Good job Glen. Now, tell me what would bring Jaap running back here?'

Glen thought for a moment and replied, 'Andre.'

'Andre,' Karen and Sam said at the same time.

'When Andre ditched his father it ripped him apart. He sees Andre as his possession. That is why I have lived with him all these years.'

Karen and Sam exchanged glances.

Glen continued, 'Jaap wants to know everything that Andre does. Everything. It's almost an obsession.'

Sam had the makings of a solution, 'Thanks Glen. You go and rest up. We need to figure out how to get things moving.'

They moved Glen to one of the bedrooms and Sam and Karen got to work on bringing Lana and Marcus up to speed on the happenings.

Everyone was devastated at the news about Dineo. The latest word from the hospital was that he would be able to be discharged within a couple of days, and the recommendation was that he should travel back to the UK at the earliest opportunity. Karen had her phone on the coffee table and the output on speaker.

'We have to get Jaap over here. I must fulfil my promise to Dineo, he has to see Jaap face to face,' said Sam

Lana replied, 'That's going to be a tall order Sam.'

'We believe we have a way, but it's going to involve Andre.'

Lana replied, 'He doesn't want anything to do with his father, I doubt he would agree if it meant meeting him.'

'He may not actually have to meet with him Karen.'

'Sounds interesting.'

'Okay, guys, leave that one with me. Karen and I are going to bring Sergeant Thompson in on things here. In the meantime, don't mention anything to Andre. We can involve him later if we have to.'

Sam understood the kudos that would come with the discovery of the Vaalrivier operation. With what he had on the phones and his laptop, it would lead to many high profile arrests across Australia. Sergeant Thompson was being lined up for a meteoric rise to fame, and that was Sam's bargaining card to bring in the conditional arrangements that he wanted.

Sam outlined his thoughts to Karen, 'We have to establish a way to get Jaap to travel back to Perth, just telling him that Andre wants to meet with him won't be sufficient. It has to look like there is no alternative.'

'What about a car accident, we can say Andre is in hospital and is seriously ill?'

'Good idea Karen, but there are ways to check if that is true. It is very likely that Jaap may have connections in the police force.' Sam thought for a moment and said, 'What if we get Glen to say that Andre has overdosed?'

'Do you mean a suicide attempt or a drugs overdose?'

'It may work best if we are not that definitive. Let Jaap draw his own conclusions. We can get Glen to say that he found him in a comatose state and is taking him to hospital in his car.'

'That sounds like it may work Sam. Let's check this out with Glen.'

They entered the bedroom where Glen was resting and ran the scenario past him.

Glen gave it a thumbs up, 'How about I tell Jaap that Andre has been talking about him a lot lately, reminiscing about his childhood and times growing up on the farm. If Jaap thinks he is at the centre of this, it will make it more believable.'

'Can you carry this off Glen?' Sam asked.

'I have to.'

Sam asked Karen to call her friend the Sergeant and get him to come around to her place as a matter of urgency. It took them an hour and a half to finish briefing the Sergeant. Sam thought that Sergeant Thomson looked shamed that such an operation could be happening on his patch without him suspecting a thing.

Goran's gun, the laptop and the phones were on the coffee table in front of them.

'This puts me in a difficult situation Sam, you are presenting this to me now and it is my duty to act immediately. Coupled with the fact that you have no authority to act the way that you have, I should really be taking you in.'

'Here's my offer Sergeant. Jaap is the key figure in all of this, without him in custody you may find it difficult to establish links to the organised crime gangs he is involved with. You need him. If you act now, it's my bet that he will go underground. If your decision hinges on taking me in, that's fine. But on one condition, you allow Dineo and I to have a private short audience with Jaap.'

Sergeant Thompson thought for a while and responded, 'You're right Sam. But the fact remains that you have shot a man and kidnapped another.'

Sam looked at the gun and pulled out his ace card. 'That is Goran's gun. I came across it when I discovered two men on a country road late last night. They were both lying by a red Lamborghini, which you will now find parked by the entrance to the farm. I got out of my car to investigate and saw that the younger man had been wounded. The other man was extremely drunk and out of it. The gun was lying next to him. I picked him up and placed him in the boot of my car, as my first care and attention was to get the other one to hospital, which I did around 1pm this morning.'

'That is exactly what had happened Sergeant Thompson,' said Glen as he watched from the hallway leading to the bedrooms.

'And I suppose he shot you because you had told him you wanted out and were going to the police to tell them about Vaalrivier?' added Sam.

'Too bloody right mate,' said Glen.

'And you will both make statements to that effect?' asked the Sergeant.

Glen and Sam both nodded in the affirmative.

'Then I must thank you for your civic duty Sam,' said Sergeant Thompson.

'And my request for time with Jaap?'

'Granted.'

'Okay Glen, let's prepare you for this phone call,' said Sam.

CHAPTER TWENTY FIVE

Jaap was feeling very pleased with himself. It had taken him years, but his son had eventually come running to him. He always knew it would happen. His chartered jet was due to arrive at Jandakot Airport in twenty minutes time. He went to the bathroom, he had to look his best. He thought he was still an attractive man, the grey flecks of hair around his ears gave him a distinguished look, he thought. He liked the way he looked.

Sam and Dineo were already at the airport. Dineo had been discharged from the hospital in Narrogin the previous afternoon. Sam wheeled Dineo into the small private arrival room that adjoined the main arrivals section of the airport.

Andre was spending the day with Lana, Marcus and Karen. His mother had told him that she needed him around. He was oblivious to everything that had gone on and also had no idea as to what was about was to happen.

The small jet landed on time and taxied around to its holding point near to the main section of the airport. The door opened and Jaap walked down the short set of steps, where an escort met with him and directed him to the small private arrival room.

He said to the escort, 'I ordered a limo to pick me up at the plane, where is it?'

The police officer posing as the escort replied, 'Apologies sir, it's about four minutes away. Apparently, it was delayed due to an accident ahead of it on the road in. You will be comfortable in here until it arrives.'

Jaap looked at his watch and stepped towards the door as his escort opened it for him. As he walked in, the escort closed the door from the outside. Jaap noticed the two men to his right as he stood and waited to be picked up.

Sam rolled the wheelchair so it was about one metre away but directly in front of Jaap. Dineo pushed himself out of his wheelchair, he wanted to stand tall to look at this man. Jaap looked at them both in turn, wondering why this man was standing in front of him.

He snarled at them, 'What is this, who the hell are you people?'

Dineo stood firm and said nothing, he just kept staring into the eyes of Jaap. Jaap was about to speak again and stopped himself as he returned Dineo's stare. Sam stood ready to intervene if he had to. Dineo maintained his stare, never breaking contact with Jaap's eyes.

Slowly Jaap's mouth widened and he broke into a smile, 'Well well.'

Those were the only words he spoke as he recognised Dineo.

Sam lifted his phone and said, 'We are done, thank you.'

Six armed police officers entered the small room, three from each doorway. Sergeant Thompson made the formal arrest. At precisely the same time, a huge Police Tactical Group were conducting the raid at Vaalrivier.

Dineo and Sam stood in silence in the small room. Dineo broke the silence. 'Well well,' he said, and they both laughed until they almost cried.

They made their way outside to watch the police contingent drive away from the airport.

Sam called Karen and put his phone on speaker so Dineo could hear, 'It's done Karen.'

Karen relayed the message to Lana and Marcus and the response was loud applause and roars of approval.

Glen was totally bemused. 'What's going on mum?'

Lana replied, 'You may need to sit down son. There's a bit of explaining to do.'

Lana took the phone from Karen and spoke to Sam. 'Please hurry here guys. We are all waiting for you.'

Sam and Dineo made their way to Mandurah. It wasn't until Sam pulled up outside Lana's place that he realised that he had left Dineo's wheelchair in the small arrival room.

Dineo witnessed him looking for it and said, 'Don't worry Sam, I don't need that thing, not today anyway.'

Lana made a beeline for Dineo as she saw them arrive, she didn't say a word, just hugged him as she wept on his shoulder.

———

There was an air of sadness at Perth International Airport as Lana, Marcus, Karen and Andre waived farewell to their newfound friends.

'Safe travels you two and keep in touch. Okay?' Karen shouted as they walked through to passport control.

Sam shouted back, 'Karen, get Andre to tighten up your security on Facebook.'

Chapter Twenty Six

Deep down inside, Glen knew this was not going to be an easy ride. The magnitude of what he was involved in was too great. Sergeant Thompson had known Glen since he was a nipper, and apart from some minor teenage nonsense, he had no reason to think badly of him. On the contrary, Glen was generally well respected in the town for his prowess at football, he had been a star full forward for his school team for several of his teenage years.

Sam was correct in his assumption that Sergeant Thompson's star would rise as the discovery of Vaalrivier unfolded and the domino effect of that hit the criminal underworld that was tied up with it.

Unfortunately for Glen, there was a ceiling on the influence and control that Sergeant Thompson commanded in his position in the West Australian Police Force.

Accolades were up for grabs, and Narrogin became engulfed with top brass from the Force, as well as politicians looking to publicly endorse themselves with self-centred glory masked as high moral standing. The Sergeant had managed to keep Glen locked away from Goran in the holding cells at Narrogin Police station.

Sergeant Thompson visited Glen, 'Look mate, there is no easy way to say this.'

Glen felt the panic rise in his stomach, 'Shit, I don't like the sound of that.'

'This thing has gone exponential, the timing could not have been worse mate.'

'Timing of what Sergeant?'

'The death of young Ruby Fisher.'

'Sorry, I am not with you.'

'While you were in hospital getting your wound seen to, they brought her in. She had overdosed on some of the shit you and your mates were producing in your factory.'

Glen was genuinely shocked, he had known Ruby since she was born. Her family were neighbours of his mother. He dropped his head and stared at the floor in front of him.

Without lifting his stare he asked, 'What do you mean when you say it's gone exponential?'

'The State Premier is milking this for all its worth, he is vowing to make an example of those involved.'

'But I told you I want to help bring them down, I will tell you everything I know.'

'And I have passed that up the line Glen. They are talking about moving you down to Perth this evening. I just thought it was fair that you know what's going on.'

Glen raised his head to make eye contact, 'So what can I do, I mean, how do I move forward with this?'

'It's fairly certain you will be handed over to the organised crimes division. You have to let them know as soon as possible that you want to turn and be a witness for the State and that you want to make a deal.'

'And they will go for that?'

'In all honesty I don't know mate, but I hope so for your case.'

'Is that all? Is there anything else you want to tell me?'

'Your mother is here, do you want to see her?'

'No way,' then he paused and said, 'Yes, tell her I will see her.'

A few minutes later, Glen was moved to a small room where he had a supervised visit with his mother.

She was sitting at a table and crying.

As he walked in she asked him, 'Why Glen, why?'

He answered her question with a question as he turned to leave the room, 'Why did you let him have such a hold over my life?'

It was more than twenty years since 'bent cop Mick' had helped stitch up Jaap. He had done really well for himself since then. He was a senior detective in the organised crime squad and had maintained a sparkling reputation on both sides of the law. His burner phone had been ringing hot since the raid at Narrogin and the lifting of Jaap at Jandakot.

The Freo old guard, Branko and Kris had long since passed away and with Goran incarcerated it was Luka that had to make the decisions to ensure maximum damage limitation for the Fremantle Mafia.

Luka called Mick, 'When are they going to be moved?'

'Their transport is on its way to Narrogin now, it should turn around and get back to Perth at about 8pm tonight.'

'Are they being transported together?'

'Yes, at the same time, but they will be in separate vans. Don't expect anything to happen during the journey, it's beyond my control.'

'What is our best opportunity then?'

'Overnight at the holding cells in Perth.'

'Okay, just get it done Mick.'

'Go easy there mate, you owe me big time if we pull this off.'

'There will be no 'if' about it mate.'

'Okay, but it will cost you.'

'Sure Mick let's talk about that after the event. Yes?'

'Okay, no worries mate.'

———

Glen came face to face with Goran for the first time since they parted company and their plan started going pear shaped. They caught sight of each other and Goran nodded to him before they were bundled into separate paddy wagons.

Word had already got to Goran that the young bloke was about to turn. As for Glen, he had no idea of the depth or breadth of the corrupt pool that embodied his Mafia, the Police and a handful of State and Federal Politicians. He was aware that it existed, but maybe just as well for him he had no clue that it was already conspiring against him and his desire to save himself.

The transfer would take just over two hours and it gave him plenty time to reflect on how foolish he had been. He had revelled in the money and the buzz that went with his illicit lifestyle, but he had paid little thought as to how it affected others. The face of Ruby kept coming into his thoughts. Whatever it took, he had to come good and do the right thing.

Glen knew what he had to say when the opportunity arose. It was getting late now and he thought his chance would come in the morning. He looked around the tiny cell, dropped his face into his hands and cried for the first time since the funeral of his father.

He didn't hear the door to his cell open at 3am. He didn't feel the bed sheet being tied around his neck. He did see the two men as they lifted him up and tied off the bed sheet to the bars on the window at the back of the cell. He could not scream or call out as he was already choking.

Glen was pronounced dead at 4:30am, after being found hanging in his cell following a routine check.

Sergeant Thompson felt physically sick when he heard the news of Glen's suicide. He knew Glen was distressed, but he thought the lad was coming to terms with things and was in a good place to move forward with the plan they had devised together. As it was only a matter of time before the media got hold of the news and published yet another death in custody story, he felt he had to let Karen know as soon as possible.

Karen smiled as she noticed Sergeant Thompson walk into the cafe, 'Good morning local hero.'

'Can we have a word Karen?'

Karen led him over to a quiet table in the corner of the cafe.

'What's up mate?'

'It's not good news Karen, they found Glen hanging in his cell in Perth. It's looking like suicide at this point.'

Karen was deeply saddened, in spite of everything that Glen had been involved with she still saw him as a nice young kid. 'This is terrible news. How could this of happened?'

Sergeant Thompson just shook his head and did not respond further to her question. 'Sorry Karen, I have to go. There is much to do. Jaap has a hearing today and I have to attend court for that. Can you please let Lana, Marcus and Andre know what has happened?'

'Of course, thanks for letting me know,' replied Karen as she kissed him on the cheek.

With Glen out of the way, Jaap's chances of avoiding a conviction were looking better and better. Jaap instructed his brief to go for the throat of anyone he could to diminish his involvement in anything illegal.

His lawyer would argue that his arrest was based on guilt by association. After all, Jaap had sold the farm and had nothing to do with it beyond the sale. Yes, there was a link with McGuire Agricultural Holdings, but he ceased to be a director of that company when the agricultural machinery division folded years ago. Any activities that were currently taking place at the farm were under the governance of the owner, Sandra McGuire. His business bank accounts showed that all income was generated through his Consultancy in International Logistics.

His brief was also keen to point out that any texts, emails and social media messaging would not stand the test of reliability. It would be so easy, for a small fee, for anyone to recruit a hacker to frame his client. Mr. Van NieKirk was deeply saddened by the unfortunate suicide of Glen. But the fact remained that the act of taking his own life proved that the young man was extremely unstable. Furthermore, anything that he had said, or may have said had he lived, could not be taken as credible.

Based on these facts, Jaap's lawyer made an application for bail which was granted and set at Aus$1,000,000.

Jaap had spent one night in a holding cell before being granted his liberty.

As for the confrontation at Jandakot airport, it appeared that his arrest was not connected to any historical events in South Africa. No charges had been levelled at him that led back to Dineo in any way. Jaap concluded that Dineo and the Englishman were content to see him apprehended in association with his current criminal activities.

It was a shame, he thought, that the old black man was not still around to watch him walk free.

———

Sergeant Thompson called Karen, 'There is more bad news. Jaap has made bail.'

———

Jaap called Luka from a public telephone, 'Meet me on the Rottnest Ferry, 1pm sailing.'

Three hours later and Luka had positioned himself so he could see the gangway from his seat and watched as Jaap came onboard the ferry as the last passenger. Jaap entered the main interior passenger area and took a seat two rows in front of Luka. After five minutes Luke joined him, which was the confirmation that Jaap was not being tailed.

'So, what is the state of play Luka?'

'We are doing everything we can for Goran, but it's not looking good for him. He is holding fast at keeping silent and knows he will have to take the hit on some serious time inside, it's the only way to protect our people in Melbourne. It's much the same with Sandra, her footprints are on everything. That's the way we set it up though, so no surprises there. She won't talk.'

'Did Glen talk before we took care of him?'

'Apparently not.'

Jaap smiled, 'Then where are we vulnerable?'

'Just Mick. He is starting to get a little greedy.'

'Is he? In what way?'

'He reckons that we owe him big time.'

Jaap laughed, 'Does he now?'

The ferry took only 30 minutes to arrive at the small tourist Island that sits just offshore from the City of Perth. After disembarking, they made their way to a cafe overlooking one of the quiet sandy bays populated with yachts and pleasure crafts.

As the waiter finished pouring their wine Jaap suggested, 'Maybe we should oblige our friend Mick. What is likely to satisfy his taste Luka?'

'Well he has the house, the car, but not the boat.'

Jaap pointed out into the bay in front of them, 'I think we need a place like this for him to take delivery of his new boat Luka, maybe somewhere a little quieter though.

What do you say?'

'I think that is a top idea mate,' replied Luka.

✿

CHAPTER TWENTY SEVEN

Rustenburg, South Africa.
Early July 2018

It took Kees Coetzee sixteen years to drink himself to the point of suicide. The alcohol had helped to maintain his lies and to mask the shame he carried for what he had done.

Within six months of Amy's death, he was drinking excessively and missing days at work. Things would get steadily worse until the mine could no longer stand by him. The sympathy eventually ran out when a fellow worker almost died in an accident that Kees had caused through his negligence. His marriage to Nadine was all but over, although she stayed with him until the end. Not only because she respected her wedding vows, but deep down inside, she still loved him.

Kees had waited until he was home alone one evening and had taken his own life on the porch at the rear of their property. Nadine had never opened his suicide note, there was no need, she already knew why he had shot himself. She discovered the note on their bedside cabinet and hid it immediately. That note may have helped the police with their investigation into his death, but his personal difficulties were very well known to the Rustenburg police as it happened, and all the evidence they gathered confirmed it was suicide anyway.

—⁓—

The seven Bakkies involved in the massacre carried seven gunmen, seven drivers and one passenger, Kees. Kees chose to ride with his friend Jaap on that day.

—⁓—

On the anniversary of Kees's death, Nadine would recover the photograph from its hiding place. She would look at the image of her husband, Jaap and their driver, Steyn, and recall the mixed emotions of anger and pride that she felt at the moment she took the picture. They were on their way to avenge the death of her child. Jaap was the mastermind of the plan and insisted on being in the lead vehicle. He looked so proud of himself as he held his gun up for the photograph.

—⁓—

Amy had an older sister Anna. Anna had given birth to a beautiful baby girl one year after the tragic death of her father. The child was the reason that Nadine carried on. She adored her granddaughter Amy. Amy was clever, very pretty and a caring person. She was also very active in a movement that helped to raise international awareness about the senseless murders of white farmers in South Africa. It was through that organisation that she learned of the arrest of an expatriate South African businessman in Australia. His parents were murdered recently during a farm attack. An associate had shared the information on a forum in the event that someone may have known him and felt the need to correspond with him in regard to the sad loss of his parents.

Amy found an online link to the newspaper story about Jaap's arrest, showed it to her grandmother and asked, 'Ouma, do you know this man?'

Nadine read the article and told Amy that she did know him, but that man had left South Africa many years ago and she had not seen him in such a long time.

'Should we contact him? You knew his parents very well didn't you?'

'Ya honey, but I am not sure it would do any good for me to get in touch with him.'

'Okay Ouma, I thought it would be interesting for you to see anyway.'

'Ya Amy, it was, and I thank you for sharing it with me.'

This revelation disturbed Nadine, for two nights afterwards she had vivid nightmares about the massacre. On the second night after awaking in a cold sweat, she decided to retrieve the suicide note and read it.

Nadine, my love

I am so so sorry that things have ended this way, but it is impossible for me to go on any longer. My conscience has tortured me for so long.

Nadine, you have stood by me all this time but there are things I have not shared with you. As hard as I tried to, I could not find it in myself to tell you.

But now is the time and I am so ashamed of myself for doing it in this cowardly way. Amy was not killed by the driver of the truck, I blamed him.

I was already in a foul temper about something that happened at work and when he refused to move his vehicle, I went into a rage. I wanted to show him who was boss, so I rammed his truck. I was so focused on dealing with him and I did not realise that Amy had got out of the Bakkie. I took the life of our darling child. I don't know why I got so angry that day and it really doesn't matter because there is no excuse for how things turned out.

Once I realised what I had done I panicked and after that everything happened so fast. I went straight to Jaap after the accident, I wanted him to help me, I needed his advice. He took charge. At first we were only going to track down the driver, but we could not find him. We found his abandoned vehicle but he was long gone. It was then that Jaap said we should take revenge in the town. He said we had to send them a strong message. I went along with it because I didn't want anyone to know I had taken the life of my little girl.

So many people have suffered because of me and my actions. I have thought many times about confessing my wrong doing, but a lot of people were involved in the cover up of the killings in town and I did not want to go against them. You and Anna may not have been safe if I had.

By the time you read this letter it will be all over for me, but I want you to know the truth.

I never meant for the massacre to occur the way it did. If we had found the driver, then only one life would have been taken and looking back that would not have been right either. But I had started something I could not stop.

I am sorry for the misery I have brought to our family and to everyone involved.

I hope one day that you and Anna can begin to forgive me.

I love you, I am so sorry
Kees

Nadine read the note over and over. She was devastated that he had kept this from her. For all these years she had believed that her daughter was killed by the truck driver. Why didn't he tell her? Why did he go running to his friend? She had never really liked Jaap, she had seen though his false charm. She took out the photo again and looked at the image of Jaap. He was smiling, Kees was not. Now she understood why the attack at the bus station had been so violent. Jaap was using the situation to inflict pain and suffering for his own satisfaction. He wanted to be the big man.

She made some coffee and, as morning broke, she called Anna and asked her to come over with Amy. They had to know the truth.

The girls arrived at 8:30 am.

Anna asked, 'This sounds serious, what's happened mum?'

'There is something important that I have to discuss with you, it's about Kees.' She pointed at the note on the table in front of them. 'That is the note he left when he took his life. I opened it for the first time today.'

The girls looked at Nadine to encourage her to continue.

'I didn't open it before now because I thought I knew why he killed himself. Nadine handed them the photograph and pointed to Jaap. 'But when Amy spoke to me a couple of days ago, she mentioned this man.'

Amy touched the photograph and asked, 'Is that Jaap VanNieKirk?'

'Ja, when my Amy was killed, Kees went to him. He always looked up to Jaap and thought he would know what to do. Kees wanted Jaap to help him track down the driver. I have to tell you now that there are things that I have kept from you. Please understand I only did that because I wanted to protect you.'

The girls started to look worried, Anna took Amy's hand.

Nadine continued, 'There is no easy way to say this, but Kees was involved in a terrible, vengeful, mass killing.'

The girls began to weep and Anna simply said, 'Mum.'

'In this note he says that he did not want things to go that far. He thought they were only going to find and punish the driver. But when they couldn't find him, Jaap had another plan.'

'Why didn't we know of these killings Mum?' Anna asked.

'We were all sworn to silence, it was a dark secret. Many people were involved. You have to understand that things were very different then to how they are now. Believe me, it has not been easy for me to keep my silence for all of these years.'

Nadine started to cry and the girls crossed over to her and hugged her.

Nadine was struggling to tell them of the rest of Kees's confession, 'It may be best if you read this.' She handed it to them. 'Please read it together.'

Anna laid the note out on the table in front of her and Amy. Nadine watched on as her girls tried to absorb the horror of the revelation. When they finished reading, none of them spoke, they simply sat in shock and looked at each other for what seemed an age. Then they cried together as a family.

CHAPTER TWENTY EIGHT

Nadine's girls stayed with her for the rest of the day and overnight. There was no way they could leave her on her own after reading the things they had in the suicide note.

Over breakfast Nadine declared to them, 'We have to find a way to notify the authorities about Jaap's involvement in these murders.'

Anna said, 'That's exactly what I think Mum. Dad did a terrible thing, but that man took it to another level. We have lost everything and by all accounts he has done very well for himself, well at least up to now.'

Amy commented, 'I couldn't sleep much last night, so I tried digging up what I could on him. It looks like the charges may not stick. He is out on bail and the body of blame is being aimed elsewhere. His big shot lawyer is claiming he has been framed.'

'Then we have to be very careful how we manage this,' said Anna.

Luka had organised the boat. He would pick it up at Fremantle marina and prepare everything as instructed by Jaap. The medium sized power boat was built to impress, ideal for water sports and fishing and its new owner Mick would be absolutely delighted with his new toy.

Mick had been instructed to meet Luka at Salmon Bay, Rottnest Island, where he would wade out in the shallow waters to take delivery of his gift. Jaap would arrive by ferry one hour earlier and Luka would pick him up from a jetty.

—⁂—

The dilemma faced by Nadine was how to ensure that the evidence she had about the massacre could be used effectively to incriminate Jaap and lead to his prosecution. Where would she start and who could she trust? There was of course her own culpability to consider also. She was prepared for the worst, if there was a price to pay to bring Jaap to justice and to help clear her conscience, then so be it.

—⁂—

The terms of Jaap's bail allowed him a liberal amount of free movement. He had to reside in the Perth metropolitan area and was required to report into Fremantle Police station three evenings a week.

It was a beautiful crisp sunny morning when Luka picked him up on the jetty. Jaap boarded and inspected the wetlines that Luka had set, they would be baited prior to picking up Mick at Salmon Bay.

'Let's take her for a spin Luka, we have a little time to kill.'

'Sure Jaap, anywhere in particular you want to go?'

'No, not really. Oh, do you mind if I take the controls? I may need a bit of a lesson though.'

'No problem mate.'

Jaap loved the feel of taking control of the boat, the power in his hands.

—⁓—

Amy was an empath and ultra protective of her Ouma. She worried that the photograph and the suicide note would corroborate a case against Nadine and at the same time may not be credible enough to convict Jaap. There was a huge risk in stepping forward with a plan to use them.

Amy spoke to her mother about her concern, 'Mum, please ask Ouma to hold off until I check out some options.'

'What do you have in mind?'

'I have access to some legal people through the movement I am involved with. I am thinking we can ask them to look at a hypothetical situation for us. They may also know who we can trust.'

'That sounds fine Amy. I will tell mum to sit still in the meantime.'

—⁓—

It was time to go pick up Mick. Jaap set the bait on the hooks of the wetlines and Luka took over the controls and headed towards Salmon Bay. Jaap moved down to the small cabin below decks, Mick did not need to know that he was onboard.

Jaap had a good view from the porthole and used the binoculars to locate Mick on the beach. He was alone, as briefed. Jaap zoomed in on his face and picked up the broad smile at the very moment that Mick realised that this was going to be his boat.

Jaap had not discussed his plan with Luka, that was always the working arrangement. Luka simply followed Jaap's instructions, it had been that way for many years now.

―――

Amy had some information to share with her mum and Nadine, 'Okay, here we go. It will be possible to extradite Jaap back here to South Africa. Once the case is built against him, a formal request will be made to return him to face charges here.'

Nadine placed her hand over her mouth and exclaimed, 'So, he will return to South Africa?'

'Yes Ouma, any trial would be here.'

Anna asked Amy, 'How does this affect mum?'

'I posed the query hypothetically to the legal folks and the response was that there is a strong case that Ouma could ask for immunity from prosecution because she was not directly involved. The fact that there was manipulation by 'others' to cover things up would also help. But she would have to name names.'

Nadine asked, 'So there is a good chance we could bring Jaap to justice?'

'Yes, but there has to be a strong body of evidence for the authorities to even think about going after him.'

―――

Mick was so excited, he didn't wait for the boat to come right into the shallows, he swam out fully clothed to get onto the craft as soon as he could.

'Well fuck me dead, this is awesome mate,' he shouted to Luka as he climbed up the rope ladder on the side of the boat.

'She's a beauty and she's all yours mate,' replied Luka.

Mick moved round the deck and settled at the sitting area at the aft of the boat. Luka nodded over to the wetline rigs and said, 'Thought we might go out a little and try out the gear.'

'Sounds bloody good to me mate,' smiled Mick.

Luka pulled back on the dual throttles and the boat blasted forward thrusting Mick hard into his seat. As the boat settled into a comfortable cruising speed, Jaap emerged from the cabin below carrying three ice cold beers.

Mick was a little tense when he saw him, but relaxed when Jaap smiled and said, 'I couldn't miss this moment Mick. I thought it would be good to thank you personally.' 'I am lost for words Jaap,' said Mick as he took the beer from Jaap and shook his hand.

'Take a seat and enjoy the ride on your boat Mick, you deserve it man,' replied Jaap as he joined Luka at the control consul.

'Where to Jaap?' asked Luka.

'Take her a few miles out, just make sure we are alone.'

Luka nodded and turned on the radar.

Jaap stepped down and took a seat next to Mick, 'So man, how water tight are we?'

'Pretty tight Jaap.'

'What's that mean?'

'Well, it's fair to say that there are no loose cannons out there. I've tightened everything around myself. We are pretty well locked down.'

'And the case against me?'

'Your brief has done a great job, it looks like they are on the verge of dropping the charges against you. If it goes to trial, it's likely to fall apart quickly.'

Jaap smiled and patted Mick on the shoulder, 'How about another beer mate?'

Nadine pondered overnight on what her granddaughter had discussed with Anna and her. She came to the conclusion that it was time to act. Since the loss of Amy and her husband, so much had changed. Some believed that the current level and direction of violence was retribution for past sins and that it was justified. But Nadine truly believed the only way forward was to stop prodding at the sore and allow it to heal. For the first time, she felt she had a chance to help deliver some form of atonement, she loved her country and believed in it. She summoned the girls to talk about the next move.

Nadine asked Amy, 'So who do we trust with this?'

Amy smiled at her grandmother as she replied, 'I am quite close to the legal people I spoke with Ouma, I think they saw through my hypothetical example because one of them gave me a business card to give to my friends, should they need any help. I believe we can trust them.'

'But aren't these people more concerned with the murders of white farmers and the expropriation program that's going on?' asked Anna.

'They are first and foremost compassionate people Mum, that's a quality that works in all directions.' Nadine smiled and touched the hand of her granddaughter, she was very proud of how she had grown up.

Luka pulled back on the throttles and spun the boat around at the same time. The boat rocked slowly from side to side and settled on the gentle sea swell that was occurring about four miles offshore.

'How about we check out these wetlines Mick?' asked Luka.

Luka and Mick made their way over to the fishing rigs, as they did so Jaap went to the leeward side of the boat and tipped two buckets of fish bait into the water. Then he joined the others and asked Mick, 'So, what's the verdict mate?'

'She's a beauty Jaap, a real beauty.'

The only sound to be heard was the water lapping against the side of the boat.

Mick was busy reeling in the line when Jaap lifted him by the right leg and pushed him overboard.

As first Mick thought it was a joke and shouted up to Jaap, 'Good one mate. The old tricks are the best.'

Jaap said nothing and just delivered a cold stare back at the bent cop.

'Come on mate, throw the ladder over. I get the joke, but let me back up.'

Jaap continued with the stare and Mick slowly realised that this was no joke.

The panic started to set in and Mick shouted. 'Come on Jaap, I've done everything you asked, told you everything, and I've kept a tidy shop for you all these years mate. What's going on?'

Jaap saw the first fin appear on the leeward side of the boat close to the bait and blood floating near the surface. He turned to face Luka, 'What do you say Luka, can we trust this guy?

As Jaap asked the question he pulled the gun from the back of his shorts and shot Luka right between the eyes.

As Luka dropped like a stone Mick shouted, 'Jaap mate, what's wrong, what's going on?'

Jaap lifted Luka up and threw him overboard on the leeward side. Within a few seconds three fins were circulating around him.

Mick tried to grab hold of the engines at the rear of the boat and get some purchase so he could climb back up. Jaap ran to the control panel and started the engines, which in turn cut into Mick's feet. Jaap edged the boat forward and pulled away, so he could view the two bodies in the water, bleeding and drawing the attention of the gathering tiger sharks.

Mick was screaming, probably down to a combination of his injuries and fear of the tiger sharks. The sharks had already started nudging the lifeless body of Luka.

'Don't leave me mate, please don't leave me.' These were the last words that Jaap heard from Mick as he throttled the engines and set the course back to Fremantle.

Jaap abandoned the boat in the harbour, as close as he could to the spot where he had once boarded a yacht and been the victim of an elaborate stitch up by Luka, Mick and their associates.

꙰

CHAPTER TWENTY NINE

Brighton early July 2018

Since their return, Sam was paying daily visits to Dineo. His friend was having good days and bad days but was generally in great spirits. Dineo had given him a key to the apartment but Sam preferred to knock and wait for his friend to answer. He had been knocking for several minutes but with no response. Eventually he opened the door and entered. Dineo was lying on the bed. Sam walked over and touched his brow, it was cold. The old man must have passed away peacefully in his sleep. Sam knew it would only be a matter of time, but his heart sank just the same.

He saw the airmail envelope on Dineo's bedside cabinet, it had been opened but there was nothing in it. He looked around the small bedsit and spotted the pages of the letter tucked behind the clock on the mantlepiece. He walked over, picked them up and sat at the table that was next to the window of the apartment to read though them.

It was a hand written letter from Lana.

My Dear Friend Dineo

I do hope you are well and have recovered from any jet lag that you may have had after such a long journey. I have to say that we are all missing you and Sam so much. The TV news and newspapers are at bursting point with the fallout from the arrests and the discovery of the factory at the farm. The impact of your efforts has been massive.

Andre and I have made a decision. We have been totally inspired by your courage and sense of decency as a wonderful human being.

We would like you to be the first to know, well except for Karen and Marcus. (It would be impossible to keep a secret from Karen anyway!)

But we have a plan for the farm in South Africa. We are going to make it a refuge centre for women and young girls that have suffered from physical or mental abuse. It will be open to all races and ages. With your permission we would like to name it after you.

We plan on sharing our time between Australia and South Africa this year in order to start the building program and to establish it as a charitable organisation.

Nothing would give us more honour than having you there to open it for us. We are aiming for this to happen in early December this year.

No rush to reply, but please let us know in your own time. Until then God bless and give our love to Sam. (Our hero) Love and our kindest thoughts,

Lana, Karen, Marcus and Andre

Sam looked over to his friend and said, 'So glad you got to read that pal.'

―⁓―

It was midday before Sam was able to lock up Dineo's apartment and watch the ambulance take him away. It would be late evening in Mandurah and Lana would more than likely be taking a glass of red with Marcus on their balcony to watch the sunset on the Indian Ocean. It was as good a time as any to call them.

It was Marcus that picked up the phone. Sam suggested that he and Lana listen in together. As he broke the news to them of Dineo's passing, he could hear Lana weeping and the sound of Marcus trying to comfort her.

'I am sorry guys, it's been a tough day here and I thought you would want to know. By the way Lana, he had read your letter.'

That appeared to make Lana perk up, 'Oh Sam, I am so pleased.'

After a few seconds Marcus said, 'We have some news at this end Sam.'

Marcus went on to tell Sam about Glen's death and Jaap's release on bail.

'Gosh, what can I say. It's sad news about Glen. I really thought he was going to come through this and redeem himself. As for Jaap, well the only consolation is that Dineo passed away having had his moment with him. Let's hope the trial goes better for us.'

Lana asked, 'Should we come over for Dineo's funeral Sam?'

'Honestly Lana, I would say not. I have arranged everything for a couple of day's time and you have enough to deal with over there. But thanks for offering.'

Marcus asked, 'Sam, do you think we need to worry about Jaap being out on bail?'

'He wouldn't be that stupid to try anything. He will be in survival mode right now.'

Sam concluded the call and they promised to keep in touch.

It was just over four months since Sam had last visited the small church in Brighton. So much had happened in that time.

He stood alone in the front row this time and tried with his awful singing voice to keep up with the hymn this time. There was only a small turn out for Dineo's funeral and even less for the cremation, but that didn't really matter, he was there for him.

Sam looked over to the stained glass windows on the left hand side of the church. There was a ray of light, just like the one that he had seen a few months earlier shining in, and it landed on the same spot where Dineo had once stood.

CHAPTER THIRTY

Debbie reclined in the business class seat as the plane levelled out for the flight to Perth from Sydney. The air hostess presented her with a glass of Champagne and Debbie remembered why she loved Jaap so much. She touched the diamond necklace that she was wearing and smiled to herself as she looked out of the aircraft window through the billowy white clouds and down to the vast red earth openness of the Australian outback. She knew her man was innocent because he had told her so, and he was always right, he had his moments but she had never met a man like him.

Nadine looked at the lawyer, he couldn't have been much older than her granddaughter, 'Nice to meet you, and thanks for seeing me.'

'It's my pleasure Mrs Coetzee.'

'Where do you want me to start?'

'Well, Amy has given me the originals of the letter and the photograph and provided some really good background to the case.' He paused for a moment. 'I think it is only fair that I let you know that if we formally start this, there could be many twists and turns. We are not dealing with a stable and consistent police force or government here. There is a risk it could not end well for you and there are no guarantees in regard to prosecuting Mr. Van NieKirk.'

'Mr Klerk, I have been living with lies and a terrible sadness for more than thirty five years. Now I find out that the person who was responsible for taking a major role in creating that misery is now reaping more of it and likely to get away with his sick atrocities once again, I have no option other than to act.'

The young lawyer smiled with heartfelt respect at Nadine and replied, 'I will do everything I can for you.'

Debbie picked out her name on the board being held up by her limousine driver at the domestic arrivals gate. The driver took her luggage and walked her out to the parking area. He opened the door for her and she let out a short scream as she saw Jaap sitting in the car. He was holding two champagne flutes and wearing a huge smile.

As they made the short drive to the serviced apartments on the South Perth foreshore, Jaap addressed Debbie's concerns about his arrest.

'Look darling, you don't get to be as successful as I am without making a few enemies. I wasn't aware that I sold the farm to a bunch of villains. I got a good price for it and didn't ask too many questions at the time. Now they are trying to frame me by saying I was in on everything.'

'Could you end up going to jail?'

'I doubt that very much darling, my lawyer has said there is next to no chance of that happening.'

Debbie snuggled up to him and held her glass out for more champagne, 'When will you know you are in the clear?'

'The trial is set for ten days time. I would imagine it won't take long to clear my name. Then we can get back to normal life in Sydney. Now let's make the best of the time we have together and try not to think about this nonsense so much.'

Jaap was pleased with his efforts. He had seen off most of, if not all, of the serious threats that could have worked against him. Debbie was here with him now and it was important that he looked as ordinary as possible to anyone that may be looking.

—◦—

Amy and Anna agreed to protect Nadine as much as they could. Mr Klerk, or James as he preferred to be called, had told them that this may be exhausting for her and it would be better if they didn't tell her everything. They should only include her if they needed more information from her. Amy offered to do the bulk of any research needed, she loved the internet and social media platforms, so it would be a labour of love for her. She began her detective work by checking out the online articles about Jaap's arrest. While doing so, she discovered that a Sergeant Thompson had been the arresting officer. She did a little more digging on the Sergeant and found out that he was a well respected figure in the Narrogin community.

James picked up his phone, 'Hi, howzit Amy, what have you managed to find out so far?'

'There is quite a bit of noise on social media that Jaap will not end up being prosecuted. Looks like he has some clever people around him.'

James tried to reassure her, 'That won't have any impact on our pursuit of him though.'

'Yes, but what if he gets off and goes to ground somewhere?'

'Okay, I get your point.'

'Would it be inappropriate for us to contact the Australian police directly in regard to our man Jaap and his crime here?'

'No, that would be fine, but charges would have to be laid here first.'

'There appears to be an ordinary decent cop involved with his arrest over there and we can easily reach him. Would it hurt to alert him that we are going after Jaap?'

'I don't see why not, we won't be committing a crime by doing so. But let's get the ball rolling at this end first.'

—⁓—

James assembled the Coetzee ladies the next morning and briefed them on the approach they should take. They had to report the crime at Rustenburg police station. He did not believe that they would detain Nadine, but there was a slim chance that it may happen. They all agreed it was time to go ahead.

The desk Sergeant listened to the brief account of the crime as presented by James and then he ushered them through to a small interview room. 'Please wait here, I will get someone to come and talk with you.'

Nadine sat between her girls and nervously gripped their hands. Two detectives entered the room, a black man and a white woman. James once again provided a brief outline of the crime.

The male detective responded, 'Please give us a few minutes and we will get back to you.'

As the detectives left the room Anna asked James, 'What do you think is happening now?'

'I would imagine they will be looking at records.'

They all sat in silence until the detectives returned.

The female detective opened the conversation this time. 'We are aware of an event that took place at the bus station in 1983. Our records confirm that this was essentially an act of civil unrest, a riot that unfortunately ended in multiple fatalities. No witnesses came forward and after exhaustive attempts to identify the gunmen, the case was closed after six months, due to lack of evidence to enable any arrests.'

Amy reflected on what her Ouma had said about the cover up. She looked at James and nodded for him to continue.

James took out the photograph and the suicide note and said, 'We would like to present some fresh evidence and have this case opened again.'

The detectives took a full statement from Nadine and requested that they leave things with them for the time being.

James handed them his business card, 'Please contact me in the first instance when you have some feedback for us.'

The male detective responded, 'Sure, we will be in touch in due course.'

The Coetzee ladies and James regrouped in the car park and Anna asked. 'So what now James?'

'They will pass this up the line to see if it is worthy of investigation. They will make the decision based on time, money, resources and I hope, political implications.'

'Why would you hope for a political bias?' asked Anna.

'Because it will create a political football that will allow me to get in and start kicking.'

The ladies all looked puzzled.

James continued, 'Scores of crimes are being committed against white farmers and they are happening today, but very little effort is going into solving them. This massacre was, and remains, a terrible crime, but it is historical and based on discrimination against a specific racial group. If they pursue it, then it will provide me with some political leverage to focus minds on the lack of racial equality being applied today.'

Amy stepped up to James, hugged him and kissed him on the cheek. Nadine and Anna looked on and turned to smile at each other as James blushed slightly.

It was late afternoon in Narrogin when Sergeant Thompson saw the incoming call from South Africa.

'G'day. Sergeant Thompson speaking.'

James had his phone set on speaker. He introduced himself and Amy then said, 'We are calling in connection with a man called Jaap Van NieKirk.'

The Sergeant cut them off as soon as he heard the name. 'I am sorry, but I won't be able to discuss anything about that person. I am involved in a case concerning him currently. Sorry.'

Amy cut in, 'But this is important Sergeant, he is....'

Once again the Sergeant repeated his previous words and added. 'Look, send me an email. Outline your issue with him and I will pass it on to someone so it can be looked at.'

Sergeant Thompson gave them his email and bade them farewell. Within ten minutes, he had read the contents of the email. He also owned a burner phone, it was his private opinion that if they were good enough for the crooks then surely, they were good enough for the law keepers.

He sent a text to James's number. *'Do not reply to this. Rest assured your email will go to the right place. Pursue things at your end as soon as you can.'*

Jaap and Debbie had spent a wonderful day at the races and he continued with his love bombing on his young partner with a visit to the celebrity high roller room at the casino. He had no idea that the punter at the end of the poker table was conducting surveillance on him.

Four days later and James's wish had come true. This case was deemed to have political clout by the powers that be and he received notification that the papers for extradition were being fast tracked. He called around to Nadine's modest home to break the news personally.

'Thank you James, that is such a relief. What happens now?'

'We sit still. The authorities in both countries will follow the procedure set out in a treaty we have for these types of things. Oh, by the way, I think you have to thank your granddaughter Amy more than me though.'

After seeing James out to his car, Nadine returned to her living room and sat back in her armchair. She reached over and lifted the photo album onto her lap. She opened it at the page where she had photos of both Amy's alongside each other. The photos had been taken when they were at the same age. She ran her fingers over the pictures and said out loud and to herself. 'Maybe I have to thank both of my Amy's.'

⸻

As he and his lawyer had expected, Jaap was acquitted of all charges in connection with Vaalrivier. Jaap punched the air as he walked free of the courthouse. Debbie was there to meet him, and as she ran up to greet him a hand touched her shoulder and held her back. Instead of hugging her man, she watched as he was approached by a black male detective and two armed West Australian police officers. Jaap was marched off and placed into an unmarked police car and that was the last she saw of him.

CHAPTER THIRTY ONE

Dineo was not the only survivor on his bus on the day of the massacre.

A young boy was travelling with his mother. When she was fatally wounded, she slumped over her son and provided him with protection from the onslaught of bullets. Kagiso was seven years old and he remembered everything that happened that day as if was yesterday. As a young boy, he had always loved the thought of becoming a police officer. Although at that time, his attraction was based on cars and uniforms more than anything else.

By the time he had reached the age of 16, his desire to become a police officer had developed into an obsession. His wish converted into reality when he was 22, when an opportunity presented itself to him following implementation of the affirmative action policy in South Africa.

He was now in his twentieth year of service and had made the rank of Sergeant. Kagiso was sitting at his desk and reading the handover notes from the night shift Sergeant. That was when he first learned that a prisoner was to be picked up at Johannesburg airport and transported to Rustenburg. Jaap Van NieKirk was being extradited to stand trial for a historical crime that took place in the town in 1983. Kagiso's heart skipped a beat and he could hardly contain himself as he opened the file for further reading of the actual charges. As he delved into the evidence associated with the case, he was in no doubt that this man was part of the group of white men that had murdered his mother and so many others.

More by coincidence than design, Kagiso would be the accompanying officer when Jaap would make the trip in the high security police van from the airport to Rustenburg.

Kagiso's emotions were rollercoasting as he waited on the tarmac for the handover of Jaap. His task was to secure the prisoner in the rear of the van and monitor him for the duration of the journey. Two armed police officers would travel up front and, if required, would communicate with Kagiso through a sliding window situated behind them.

Kagiso checked that the safety lock was in position on his weapon. He double checked the chains and cuffs that restrained Jaap and knocked on the adjoining bulkhead to inform the driver that everything was good to go.

Jaap wasted no time, 'You do realise that this is a complete waste of everybody's time?'

Kagiso said nothing, he kept his focus on the space above Jaap's head in a deliberate attempt to avoid eye contact.

Jaap continued and tried to make eye contact with his escort. 'Look, I know you are just doing your job. But all of this is nonsense. Trumped up charges, probably politically driven, and I am the scapegoat.'

Still no response or eye contact from Kagiso.

'Okay, okay. Listen, I am a very wealthy man. What do you make as a cop? Help me out and I will make all of your dreams come true. Surely, we can work something out. I still have friends in high places here, whatever you want we can work it out.'

Jaap was beginning to get irritated with being ignored, but tried to keep his cool. 'We could make this look like an ambush, without anyone getting hurt.'

Kagiso's stone cold look added more fury to Jaap's fiery temper, 'Look man. Times were different back then. I was only doing my bit to keep law and order. That was the way of things then. Okay, a few people got hurt but things were under control, not like now. Now let's talk about how I can help you, if you help me escape.'

Kagiso smiled as he raised his phone and turned the screen towards Jaap. He pressed the button to stop recording and placed the phone on the seat to his right.

Jaap squinted at his escort and said, 'You fucking bastard.'

Kagiso kept a stern look on his face and replied, 'It is time for you to shut up and listen. And maybe you should have listened harder when you were given your rights, 'Anything you do say may be taken down and used in evidence against you,' for example. This is my home Mr Van NieKirk, and I am proud to do my job to withhold the law and order in this country.'

'Look man, why are you taking this so personal? You don't know me, but I can make you a rich man. Everyone turns a blind eye now and then.'

'Oh, I do know you Mr Van NieKirk.'

Jaap was confused, how could this person know him?

'All of the Bakkies on that day were white, except yours. The one you travelled in was light blue.'

Jaap's mouth felt dry and he was finding it hard to swallow.

'You stopped long enough for me to see you and the two other people in that blue Bakkie before you opened fire and killed my mother. That's why this is personal,' said Kagiso as he placed his hand on his weapon.

Jaap started to shuffle in his seat and looked at Kagiso's right hand, 'You wouldn't?'

'No of course I wouldn't,' laughed Kagiso. 'You know, we don't segregate our prisoners here anymore Mr Van NieKirk. I wouldn't want to deny you the chance to reform. Besides, there will be a lot of folks you will be sharing your time with that may help you with that. Considering that most of them will be on your wavelength. Nigerian drug dealers, murderers, perhaps the rapists will also be able to show you another dimension of life and what it has to offer. You will have plenty of time to explore your options.'

Jaap's jaw had tightened and he was having palpitations. Kagiso saw the redness in his face and said, 'Now try and relax and enjoy the ride to Rustenburg.'

The van pulled into the police station in Rustenburg and the back door opened. Kagiso stood and climbed out of the vehicle and stepped away from it. A moment later he turned back towards the van and leaned in between the two armed police officers that were entering and said, 'Oh, forgive my manners Mr Van NieKirk. Welcome home.'

✿

CHAPTER THIRTY TWO

Johannesburg late December 2018

Sam gazed out of the aircraft window as it made its final approach into O.R Tambo International airport. It would only take him 25 minutes after touching down to make it through to the arrivals hall. As he finally walked out he waved over to his welcoming party.

Lana and Karen were the first to greet him, followed by Andre and Marcus. It was such a good feeling to meet with them again. They hugged and greeted each other just as all good friends do. Andre led the way to the vehicle.

They all stood back and watched for Sam to notice and read the logo on the side of the minibus.

'THE DINEO REFUGE CENTRE FOR VIOLENCE AGAINST WOMEN,' was written on the side of the vehicle.

Sam felt the emotion welling inside and couldn't speak, his heartfelt smile would have to do. They all felt his approval and happiness come across though.

History was repeating itself once again as Sam travelled on a minibus from the airport at Johannesburg towards Rustenburg.

'How long to do you plan to stay with us Sam?'

'It would be great to see the New Year in with you folks if that's okay with you?'

Karen replied, 'No bloody worries mate, it would be rude of you if you didn't.'

'Is there anything special you would like to do while you are here Sam?' asked Lana.

Sam replied, 'What time will sunset be tonight?'

Andre informed him, 'It's going to be around 7pm this evening Sam.'

'There is somewhere I need to be at that time, it's on the other side of Rustenburg. Will that be okay?'

'No problem Sam, you just show us the way mate,' said Andre.

They spent a wonderful day catching up together on the site of the old farm on the South side of the Magaliesburg mountains. The transformation of the place to become a refuge was both impressive and heart warming.

Andre suggested that it was time they were going if they were to make it to the other side of Rustenburg for the sunset. Sam remembered the way and directed them to within a few metres of where he wanted to be.

Lana, Andre, Karen and Marcus disembarked from the vehicle with him but allowed Sam to take the last few steps on his own.

They watched on as he approached the Boab tree and positioned himself in front of it. Sam looked out on to the vastness of the South African bushveld. The warm colours in the sky gave him a feeling of tranquillity. He patiently waited as the sun dropped closer to the top of the mountain on the horizon.

Sam took the lid off the casket.

The sun hit the top of the mountain and there it was, the flash of light. It only lasted a second but it was clearly visible. At that moment he scattered the ashes in front of him at the base of the tree.

He uttered the final words to his friend Dineo, 'Hamba Kashle.'

THE END

Lightning Source UK Ltd.
Milton Keynes UK
UKHW011528011219
354565UK00007B/175/P